The Art of Seduction

Sophie looked up at him with huge, trusting eyes.

William lowered his face to hers and paused for just the slightest moment. He knew from experience that pausing before a kiss heightened desire and gave the illusion to the female that he cared enough to give her a last chance to cry off. For some confounded reason he was finding it difficult to proceed.

He felt the lightest brush of cool fingertips against his cheek, like an innocent dove fluttering against him. He shuddered and closed his eyes.

All at once, he felt her tender lips brush a kiss on his cheek.

He angled his face toward her and returned the kiss, this time on her lips, barely resisting the softness he found nestled there. He resisted the urge to part his lips and crush her to him. . . .

Lord Will and Her Grace

Sophia Nash

A SIGNET BOOK

SIGNET
Published by New American Library, a division of
Penguin Group (USA) Inc., 375 Hudson Street,
New York, New York 10014, USA
Penguin Group (Canada), 10 Alcorn Avenue, Toronto,
Ontario M4V 3B2, Canada (a division of Pearson Penguin Canada Inc.)
Penguin Books Ltd., 80 Strand, London WC2R 0RL, England
Penguin Ireland, 25 St. Stephen's Green, Dublin 2,
Ireland (a division of Penguin Books Ltd.)
Penguin Group (Australia), 250 Camberwell Road, Camberwell, Victoria 3124,
Australia (a division of Pearson Australia Group Pty. Ltd.)
Penguin Books India Pvt. Ltd., 11 Community Centre, Panchsheel Park,
New Delhi - 110 017, India
Penguin Group (NZ), cnr Airborne and Rosedale Roads, Albany,
Auckland 1310, New Zealand (a division of Pearson New Zealand Ltd.)
Penguin Books (South Africa) (Pty.) Ltd., 24 Sturdee Avenue,
Rosebank, Johannesburg 2196, South Africa

Penguin Books Ltd., Registered Offices:
80 Strand, London WC2R 0RL, England

First published by Signet, an imprint of New American Library,
a division of Penguin Group (USA) Inc.

First Printing, April 2005
10 9 8 7 6 5 4 3 2 1

To
Marie-Solange Charlotte Leglise Nash
Howard, my beautiful mother, who taught
me a thing or three about
French (and American) rakes

Acknowledgments

I owe my deepest appreciation to my editor, Laura Cifelli, who believed in the powerful attraction of a very bad French rake disguised as something quite the opposite. She encouraged me not to hold back when telling his outrageous story, and for that, I am grateful. And credit must also go to Kathryn Caskie, who goaded me every step of the way despite our mutual fascination with all wicked forms of procrastination. Thank you, thank you—both of you—for making the writing of this story so pleasurable.

Chapter One

𝒜h, violets on soft flesh. Heavenly. A dizzying sensation long familiar yet always irresistible swept through William Barclay, younger son of the sixth Marquis of Granville. The lady nestling in beside him sighed softly and the bedclothes rustled and settled into place.

Oh, he was glad Miss Wynn—or was it Winter—had come to him after all. Abigails and governesses were his evening dessert of choice. They were not as vulgar as the rest of the serving class and not as jaded as the widows.

William breathed in more of her heady scent and stroked the back of her neck, twining downy tendrils in his fingers as he nipped her earlobe.

She giggled and lay still.

William smiled in the heavy darkness. He adored the innocent ones—or rather the ones who chose to play the virgin. It was amazing the little jewels of femininity one could find in the wilds of Yorkshire, far from the practiced coquettes of France, his mother's homeland.

He grasped her hand and kissed it before placing it around his back. "Ah, *ma petite chérie,* I'm so glad you changed your mind," he whispered into her ear. "I shall have to make sure you don't regret it."

He unbuttoned her night rail's front line of closures with expert dexterity and kissed her, coaxing her to soften her locked lips.

She moaned and opened beneath him like a tight rosebud unfurling in summer's heat.

He trailed kisses down her neck to the large swell of her bosom. She was better endowed than he remembered. No matter. He liked them all, small or large. Well, maybe he did prefer petite packages of femininity. But, an occasional foray into more padded fortresses could be quite satisfying too.

Long minutes passed and her breaths quickened.

A slow course of desire flowed in his veins. In the foggy sensual haze, a distant clock chimed four times.

She plucked at his back now, in mock nervousness, he was sure. "*Ma chérie,* have no fear. I won't rush you. I must have time to enjoy this glorious feast." He moved her hand to his derriere to feel her touch on his nakedness.

Another giggle escaped her lips.

Again he smiled and wished a candle burned so he could look into the abigail's lovely violet eyes that complemented her violet scent. William deftly rearranged her nightclothes for better access. He tasted her breasts, paying each of them their rightful share of attention, teasing them to tightened perfection as his hands worked their magic on her generous lower curves. Her corsets had hidden well her ample charms.

She tensed then relaxed while he massaged her hips and dared to trace the warm skin of her abdomen.

Settling one leg between hers, he kissed her soft

lips many more minutes until she seemed to almost purr. She was all pliant softness and smoldering desire.

She was ripe.

He sighed as he knew what would come next, surprise and delight mixed with a tinge of fear at his size usually. He moved her hand to the front of his body and urged her to touch him.

She gasped.

"*Mon petit chou,* it's all right, I promise I shan't hurt you."

Another shaky giggle.

Ah, thank God she wasn't naive. He didn't deflower innocents, only imaginary virgins. He contemplated prolonging the pleasurable first course of this seduction or gorging on the main feast itself. She was very good, playing the shy maiden to the letter.

The sound of a knock on his door filtered through his mind. Then the noise of many quick steps in the hallway followed. In a thrice he bounded out of the warm bed and belted his velvet dressing gown as the door to his chamber banged open with a force that exercised the hinges to the utmost.

A portly gentleman with his nightcap askew stormed into the room, a gaggle of people with candlesticks held high illuminated his passage. "What are you about, Lord Will?"

A female shriek came from behind the enraged gentleman.

"Hush, Margaret. We'll have no more witnesses to this atrocious display." The older man grabbed a candlestick from a servant, strode to the bed, and flung back the covers.

The unwed, young daughter of the house lay in

all her glory before the visitors. *Of course.* Her freckled, horselike face complemented her large girth and flanks. It would have been laughable if it had not been so tedious. At least she had re-arranged her nightclothes before her exposure.

"How dare you, my lord?" Lord Tolworth's jowls waggled back and forth like a hound on a scent. "I'll have you horsewhipped after the marriage ceremony."

"Marriage ceremony?" William replied, quietly examining his fingernails.

"You are beneath contempt, you half-French swine. I'll not like having Gallic blood in my grandchildren's veins, but I'll see you married to my Penelope even if I have to lock you in the larder for the night. You Frenchies have no notion of honor."

William looked at the large girl in his bed. He shook his head. His overindulgence in Lord Tolworth's excellent brandy last night had cost him. How could he have mistaken this rotund girl of six and ten for her pretty abigail?

"And what have you to say, Lady Penelope?" William asked.

A nicker escaped her mouth as she brushed her chestnut-colored forelock out of her eyes. "Oh, my lord, I dare not countermand Papa."

William stubbed a desire to throttle her. "Ah, I see." Caught as effectively as a fox in a well-guarded henhouse.

"You've ruined her, you feckless, hot-blooded, good for nothing slubber de Gullion."

"On my honor, Lord Tolworth, your daughter is as pure today as the day she was born, that is—as long as she hasn't made a habit of frequenting the bed chambers of other male guests."

A loutish hobbledehoy of no more than eight

and ten lumbered past Lord Tolworth. He swiped at William's jaw, but missed and almost lost his balance. "You'll meet me at dawn on the north field to avenge my dear cousin, if you have any honor whatsoever," said the young man whose heavy frame would challenge his uncle's in several years.

"Actually, I don't fancy dueling gentlemen who have yet to grow whiskers," replied William.

Lord Tolworth stepped in front of his heir. "You'll eat grass before breakfast, if you cannot find an excuse to avoid my challenge."

The father looked barely more of a test than the thickheaded nephew but at least he was well past his majority. "Oh, all right, then, if you think it really necessary. Pistols or swords, my dear sir?" William asked with a slight smile.

"Not before the wedding," cried his corpulent wife. "You promised!"

"Pistols, then—after the wedding," replied the husband, halfheartedly.

Lady Tolworth swooned into her spouse's arms. The housekeeper refused to dash away for the much needed smelling salts lest she miss any of the vastly entertaining goings-on. She patted her mistress's hands ineffectually.

William successfully stifled a laugh when he noted one of Lady Tolworth's eyes half-open and spying on him. He scratched his chin and glanced at the belligerent father. "It will be hard to comply if I am locked in your larder, my good sir. May I offer you my word of honor—as a gentleman, of course—that there is no need to keep me chilled, as a good bottle of wine, before a wedding and an affaire of honor? A watch at my door will suffice, I assure you. Unless of course your intention is to keep me like a well-preserved Spanish ham for a month while the banns are read."

"We'll not be needing the banns, my lord," Penelope said. " 'Tis but a half day's trip to Gretna Green and father will take us—just like he did when it was Ginny's turn."

William looked down to rearrange the folds of his dark blue velvet dressing gown. "You are a veritable font of information, my dear." It was fortuitous he had clothed himself in time; otherwise he would have felt a bit more guilty facing the premeditated inquisition. But then, he had always been lucky, if this situation could be described as such. He looked down at the bulging, watery eyes of the silly girl in his bed and wondered to whom he owed eternal thanks for the warning knock on his door.

Perhaps, once again, his faithful yet particular man, Jack Farquhar, had proved his weight in gold. Yes, it was to be hoped the fanciful valet could next perform miracles.

It was infernally hot in the ballroom despite the coolness of the early spring outside. A mesmerizing display of many-hued ball gowns swirled around Miss Sophie Somerset as she waltzed, making her even more dizzy than her constricting corset and the forceful embrace of her partner, Lord Coddington. She glanced about and was happy to see some of the Count and Countess of Hardwick's footmen opening the French windows and doors leading outside of the glittering ballroom. If she were not so practical she would faint from the sheer heat of it all.

Her partner's penetrating blue eyes and very pale blond, wavy hair fascinated her. He matched her height, unlike most of the other gentlemen whose noses tended to rest in her décolleté. He was decidedly the most handsome gentleman she had ever seen—a true prize among men, or at least as much of a prize as a titled gentleman with pockets-to-let could be.

But then, all the men who jotted their names on her dance card were well known to the moneylenders in town. It was the reason they asked. For what other reason would they seek an introduction to an almost on the shelf, blowsy spinster, albeit rich or very nearly rich, indeed? Sophie found it amusing how they managed to look at her with too keen an interest and yet disgust all at the same time.

Lord Coddington steered them toward the floor-to-ceiling French windows. The room seemed to tilt and become foggy as he waltzed beyond the nodding palm fronds in the planters near the closest window. Outside, they danced along the narrow balcony.

"You are one of the most attractive ladies of my acquaintance, Miss Somerset."

Before she could offer thanks, his head tilted toward hers. He was about to kiss her! *How delightful.* She closed her eyes and leaned into him to claim her first kiss. Her first real kiss—from a man to a woman—not like the ones from her papa. Suddenly, the whirling sensation ceased. She encircled her arms about his neck to more fully enjoy the sensation. Sophie relaxed into his embrace as he tightened his hold around her waist.

At first she was aware only of her breathing, of his breathing, then the sounds of the night insects humming became clearer when the music ceased. A loud buzzing grew, overtaking all other sounds. He broke away from her.

"Miss Somerset, I fear we are causing something

of a sensation," Lord Coddington whispered. "I would not blemish your fine reputation for the world. I'm sorry we cannot continue—what you so delightfully initiated. May I presume the honor of calling on you tomorrow?" His tone hinted of distaste and his smile was tight.

What? He thought she had begun the kissing?

Sophie turned in horror to find what seemed to be the entire gathering in the ballroom staring at her. What on earth was she doing next to another set of French windows? She was sure Lord Coddington had waltzed them to a deserted corner. She looked up to find him edging away from her into the ballroom with a smug expression.

A few giggles erupted from the ballroom and she noticed the cupped hands and the rounded eyes of many females gossiping and tittering in front of her.

She heard whispers of female venom, "ill-bred hoyden heiress—another exhibition of fast behavior . . ." and, ". . . gel's reputation is beyond tatters now, poor dear." Ah, revulsion she could swallow, but a true show of pity, she could not.

She was suddenly cold, colder than the frostiest winter day in Wales. She turned and tried to flee, down the steps into the garden, into the fog. Oh, she was so cold . . . and her feet wouldn't move.

Sophie woke with a start. She was freezing. All of the silk-satin bedcovers had slid off the bed and the pitch darkness proved that the fire had burned out in the hearth. She shivered and struggled to haul the covers from the floor without placing her toes on the massive bedchamber's icy cold floor. What a horrid nightmare. It had been so real. Her teeth chattered as she gathered the bedclothes tightly around her body. And then she stilled.

It had been so real, just like the ball tonight. She closed her eyes. Just *exactly* like tonight. Only she had not been able to escape from the hard, calculating stares of the crowd. Oh no, she had had to pull herself up, walk into the ballroom, where she had been unable to perceive her cousin Mari or her ancient aunt. She had stood there like a complete dolt, gawking at the many faces. She was sure everyone had been able to see her heart pounding below her inelegant bosom. It had been altogether the most embarrassing moment in her nine and twenty years.

Her only consolation was to be found in the considerable form of her aunt who suffered from very little rational conversation after consuming a vast quantity of ratafia. On this occasion, instead of chastising her niece yet again, she had chosen to sleep off her overindulgence during the whole of the miserable carriage ride back to the townhouse. Mari had been unable or unwilling to make light of the event. That had been left up to Sophie.

"So do you think it was worse tonight or did last Tuesday's disaster equal it, Mari?" Sophie rearranged the plumage of her dozing aunt's headgear that kept poking her in the face.

"Hard to say, dearest." Mari grimaced as the carriage wheel negotiated a spot of uneven cobblestones.

"So kissing in public is worse than having someone spill lemonade on me, thereby—let's see, how did that vile Lord Busby describe it? Ah, yes— 'allowing my voluptuous charms to peek through my amusing gown?' " Sophie, exasperated, removed the offending hat from her Aunt Rutledge's head as the grande dame began snoring in earnest on her shoulder.

Mari sighed and rested her forehead in her hand.

"Well, I hardly think I should have been blamed when Lord Busby was the one trying to put his hand down the front of my bodice. It's not like I wasn't trying to fend him off."

"Dearest, we've been through this before."

"I know, I know. If his wife and her circle of friends hadn't come upon us, naught would've been said." Sophie looked out the small carriage window. "Ah, Mari, come on then. You promised to cheer me up."

"Hmmm," her sweet cousin intoned, tapping her fan on Sophie's arm. "Well, it won't help at all to remind you that you shouldn't have been kissing tonight at all, public or private like, if you ask me. Especially after the old goat pawed you last week."

"Oh, but Mari, Lord Coddington was so very beautiful, don't you think? And I did so want to be kissed, at least once in my life. It was ever so interesting—until he showed his true colors that is."

"I just wish you had waited for the kisses until *after* you were married to a right and proper Londoner," Mari said. "Your nob of an uncle would turn in his grave with these goings-on and it just makes it all the harder to carry out the terms of your inheritance."

"Oh, I don't know," Sophie said, pulling up her bodice and losing the war to curb her unfashionable, full curves. "They've seen my 'charms' and know all about the possibility of a windfall. What more can they want?"

"Cheer up, dearest," Mari said, patting Sophie's hand. "There's always tomorrow. And there are all those shops we have yet to see. And after all, we've only been here a month. I'm certain you'll succeed in finding a husband."

The clock struck four, bringing Sophie back from her reverie of the evening's events. She closed her eyes and shook her head, dropping onto the downy pillows of her bed, which provided precious little comfort on the dawn of what promised to be another miserable day in London. Why, oh, why had she ever agreed to leave her beloved little village in Wales?

Sophie was struck anew with the same thought a mere ten hours later as she sat waiting for the blond perfection of Lord Coddington to mount the stairs to the morning room after being announced. Sophie shifted uncomfortably on the settee.

She and her new intimidating French ladies' maid, Mademoiselle Karine, had taken great care in Sophie's toilette and dress today. The new corset, which managed to suppress her bosom even more than the last torturous device, as well as the tight bodice of the white morning gown, constricted her lungs in a way that made it difficult to breathe. But Aunt Rutledge had insisted she wear it. Karine had looked her over from head to toe, then she had shaken her head with displeasure and muttered her opinion in French so no one could understand.

Oh, how much better and easier it was in Wales where she could wear anything she wanted as long as it was modest and serviceable. Her father had even let her wear pantaloons on the days she had been allowed to go fishing or hunting with him.

The handles on the double doors moved and a liveried footman entered and bowed with Lord Coddington on his coattails. "His lordship, miss."

Sophie rose from her perch and became light-headed. She curtsied and nodded. "My lord."

"Miss Somerset, delighted." Lord Coddington looked anything but.

"You find me alone, sir. My aunt and Miss Owens are out, paying calls."

"So the butler informed me. But as I had something particular to say, perhaps this is for the best."

Sophie felt as if she were playing a part in a bad comedy at the Drury Lane Theatre as she reseated herself on the edge of the settee. Her aunt had insisted Sophie stay behind to hear the gentleman's proposal.

Lord Coddington, playing his role to the hilt, began pacing as he gripped the edges of his tall beaver hat. "Miss Somerset, from the moment I first saw you I knew our lives were destined to become intertwined."

Sophie had the horrible urge to giggle. Her tight undergarments helped curb her initial instinct. She sighed. He was a very handsome man.

His dark blue coat accentuated his broad shoulders and just the correct amount of white froth tied in a dazzling knot appeared below his chin. His boots showed not a speck of dirt despite the rain earlier this morning.

She looked down at the tiny gravy stain on her gown from a hastily eaten meal and placed her hand over the mark. What was he saying now?

"I have been given the blessing of your aunt and my family to pay my addresses to you. But I am sure this is no surprise. And I feel I must offer for your hand in marriage to atone for the *newest* blemish on your name. Would you do me the honor then, Miss Somerset, of consenting to become my wife?"

It was clear from his proud posture, his patronizing tone and his gaze, which rested on a point just above her shoulder, that he had no feelings for her at all. She could be a codfish for all he cared as long as she brought her possible windfall to the union.

Oh yes, Miss Codfish married to Lord Coddington. A perfect match. She giggled.

"Miss Somerset? Do you find this interview amusing then? Is this your answer to my declaration?"

"No, my lord. I'm sorry if I have caused offense. I am honored by the condescension you have shown me." Sophie stopped speaking. For the life of her she did not know how to continue.

She was in London to contract an arranged marriage with a suitable nobleman of the Upper Ten Thousand. This codfish, er, gentleman was eminently qualified. But his dazzling blue eyes and light hair left her feeling unnerved.

Could she spend the rest of her life looking at his icy expression every day and, worse, perform the most intimate act with him? Surely there would be other suitable offers. But could she risk rejecting the addresses of her aunt's favorite? A gentleman who would satisfy, without question, every condition stated in the will of her late uncle, the fourth Duke of Cornwallis? The union would also fulfill the requirements of the unusual patent of nobility that allowed the duchy to be passed down to a female.

"Well, what is your answer?" Lord Coddington tapped his cane once loudly on the wide-planked wooden floor.

Sophie took a deep breath but was forced to stop midway into the effort by the unyielding undergarment. She panicked and became extremely dizzy. She prayed she wasn't going to faint, but the edges of darkness were already radiating around the edges of her vision. Oh, she was about to embarrass herself and her family yet again.

Chapter Two

"*M*ornington, by God, it *is* good to see you," William said, gripping the beefy arm of his old friend from his days at Eton. A sleepy footman eased from his shoulders a rustic, moth-eaten coat drenched from the downpour outside. "Sorry to intrude at this ungodly hour."

Charles Mornington, lord of no land, but of much wealth, looked at William and removed his off-kilter nightcap, scratched his head and tightened the belt of his dressing gown. "I can only assume that the most dire of circumstances has led you to my remote corner of the world."

"You have no idea."

"The last time you were here you swore never to set foot in this part of the country again," Mornington said.

"Necessity is the mother of—let's see—a very bad memory, shall we say?" Will raked a hand through his wet hair and smiled.

"Dare I guess this impromptu visit involves the fairer of the sexes?"

William arched a brow. "I'm not overly fond of self-incrimination, my dear friend."

Mornington looked over William's comical mixed bag of peasant clothes and turned to the footman. "Jones, be so good as to rouse Mrs. Jenkins. We'll need the blue rooms prepared and"—he glanced at William again and grinned—"one of my nightshirts and dressing gowns as it appears my good friend has arrived ill equipped."

The footman rubbed the sleep from his eyes and walked, heavy-footed, down the long hallway to the rear stairs. Mornington returned his glance to William. "So?"

"Aren't you going to offer a bit of brandy? You're not playing host very well. But I daresay I will forgive you, given the hour."

Mornington took up a candlestick and motioned the way into a dark wood-paneled library where rows upon rows of books climbed up to the vaulted ceiling. A pair of well-worn brown leather armchairs beside the padded fire railing bespoke of many comfortable hours spent in post-dinner cogitation.

"I suppose it is too much to ask for a fire?" suggested William.

Mornington sent him a glance.

"Oh, all right, I'll see to it myself," said William, kneeling down in his wet and dirty clothes to start a fire.

His former schoolmate poured amber liquid into delicate crystal glasses and brought them to the chairs.

"So?" The repeated syllable hung in the cool air.

William accepted the glass and took a long swallow before dropping into the nearest leather chair. "Well, I can safely say that even the less prudent mothers and fathers will shield their daughters from

me now. Thank God, I might add." He leaned his
wet head back and closed his eyes in weariness. "I
should have done this years ago."

"Criminy, Will. Stop the hints, and spill the tale."

With a paucity of words, he relayed his recent
encounter with the calculating Tolworth family.

"Actually, I rather think I did the family a good
turn. If I'd stayed to kill the father, I would've felt
guilty about leaving the females at the mercy of
that oafish heir." William sniffed the soiled arm of
the peasant's shirt and grimaced. "Need I assure
you I would've—well, perhaps *maybe* I would've—
married the chit if, ahem, matters had been allowed
to reach their natural conclusion?"

Mornington hid his laughter without success.
"But how did you escape?"

"With Jack Farquhar's help, of course."

"Don't tell me that peacock valet is still in your
employ? Cheekiest man alive."

"Never underestimate cheekiness."

Mornington shook his head.

"I managed to evade the larder," William continued. "But my clothes were confiscated as an in-
ducement to remain. Farquhar threw a rope up to
my window, I crept into the stables and rode hell-
bent for leather away from the blasted place."

William swallowed the remaining brandy in his
glass and idly dangled the glass from his fingers
over the arm of the chair. "Halfway to London I
traded my ring and nightshirt for these rags and
some food. Those damn Tolworths were on my
heels the entire journey. I finally lost them in the
dens of London, near the docks."

Wrinkling his nose, William pulled off his shirt
and tossed it into the roaring fire. "Excuse the in-
formality, but this has to be the most foul-smelling

rag ever. I don't suppose you've got some clothes squirreled away I could borrow?"

Mornington grinned. "What's mine is yours, my friend, although I doubt they would fit."

William perused his friend's short, hefty frame and bit back a retort. "I guess I'll have to make do with Farquhar's clothes when he arrives—that is, until I can have some clothes made up. And, by the by, a London man of business should be arriving on the morrow—along with Farquhar if the Tolworths haven't skinned him alive."

"And you think your former hosts—or should I say future in-laws—won't follow your valet?"

"If Farquhar can't outwit those Yorkshire bumpkins, I'll eat my hat—if I had one that is."

"Well, I hope you've the right of it because Anna and Felicia will be arriving in a few days and I'll not have my sisters exposed to your faux pas and *petites amies*."

"I love it when you speak French, Mornington. It shows you truly care."

"The last time Felicia saw you she behaved like a love-struck moon cow for a fortnight." Mornington studied William's bare chest. "God knows why you have that effect on females."

William laughed.

"Have a care, my friend. Lock those sisters of yours in their rooms each night for I'm tired of running, and more to the point, I've exhausted all possible hiding places." Will gratefully accepted more brandy. Once again, he closed his eyes.

"Well, I'm glad to report there's not an eligible lady for miles," Mornington said, rubbing his eyes and yawning until his jaw cracked. "Except for two recently arrived Welsh females who, according to last week's *on-dits*"—Mornington picked up an old

newspaper and scanned the page with his finger—
"yes, here it is.

" 'Miss S., of the towering frame and impressive
bosom, dissected in detail here last week, has
rightly put her tail between her legs and retreated
into the obscurity of Burnham-by-the-Sea with her
hanger-on dark cousin of lesser connections. It is
to be hoped that retirement by the sea will cure the
ill-refined female of improper conduct. Although it
is highly doubtful she will be able to reassume her
role as a marriage-minded heiress to a dukedom
given her audacious behavior and the potential resulting evidence in nine month's time. Lord C.
should be commended for his gracious efforts to
save the unrepentant miss.' "

Mornington looked up from his paper. "Good
God, I just realized, she must be the heir to the
Cornwallis title and fortune."

"Clearly the case of lost virtue and maybe worse.
The lady has my sympathies. She'll have a more
difficult time than I, repairing a reputation if it can
be done at all. Perhaps she will need comforting,"
suggested William.

"I'm sure you'd be more than happy to oblige."

"She's probably as horse-faced as the Yorkshire girl."

Mornington laughed.

"No, I've had enough scandals to last a lifetime.
Now that I'm staring at five and thirty years in my
dish, I do believe I must learn to rusticate and reform my ways."

"Wonders never cease," exclaimed Mornington,
grinning.

"That is, unless there is an opportunity, perhaps"—
William lifted an eyebrow—"one with a lilting
Welsh accent. But if there isn't a prospect for a

discreet, *simple* dalliance in the neighborhood, I'll settle for tea and giggles with your dear sisters for the remainder of the Season."

Exhilarated by the morning gallop, Sophie brought the gray mare back to a more sedate trot when she rounded the next to last turn before the beginnings of the small seaside village. The last few days had gone by with surprising ease.

Oh, there'd been the embarrassment of fainting in the midst of Lord Coddington's proposal of marriage. Worse had been facing the disappointment of her aunt when Sophie had told her she wouldn't accept his lordship's offer.

Yet Sophie had triumphed in the end by attaining her goal of a brief departure from the all-knowing, all-seeing eyes of wretched London. Aunt Rutledge called it "retrenching." Sophie didn't care what anyone called it as long as she was allowed an escape. She craved the peace of the countryside where she could dress how she liked and limit the number of people she would see.

Ensconced in the beautiful turreted mansion perched high atop a cliff overlooking the sea, she had reveled in the lonely harsh beauty of Burnham-by-the-Sea. She would never tire of listening to the cry of the peregrine falcons and the mournful cooing of the stock doves hidden in the low-lying wild thyme and horseshoe vetch. The cruel, salty winds reminded her of Porthcall.

The favored property of her recently deceased uncle, the Duke of Cornwallis, the Villa Belza had been left to her along with the other properties of the duchy with the proviso she marry a proper aristocrat, approved by the duke's sister, Aunt Rutledge. If she failed to accomplish this task by her

next birthday, the properties, wealth and title
would revert to an ancient fourth cousin, twice removed. Aunt Rutledge had appeared less than
taken with that possibility.

Sophie, intent on her errand to the linen draper,
tossed the reins into the waiting hands of the
smithy and slid from the saddle.

As she trudged toward the shop, Sophie was
aware of the stares she received by all in the little
village. The people probably found her a disappointment over the last occupants of Villa Belza.

She looked down at her cracked boots and the
frayed hem of her dusty, serviceable gown that
was two inches too short. After wearing the most
beautiful and uncomfortable clothes for the last
two months, Sophie was delighted to wear this
once again. And it hid her embarrassingly ample
bosom well—it always had. But glancing about,
she observed her gown was uglier and older than
the lowest washerwoman's rag. She felt like a
wretch.

Even the parson changed his course after one
glimpse of her. Sophie hailed him anyway.

"Mr. Seymour! I've something for you."

He turned to greet her with an embarrassed expression. "Miss Somerset. What a surprise."

Sophie reached into her pocket and removed a
coin purse. She emptied almost all of the contents
into her palm and gave him the gold sovereigns.
"You've saved me an errand. This is a donation
for the restoration of the schoolroom damaged by
the winter storms."

The parson's eyes widened at the hefty sum
placed into his hands. "Why, Miss Somerset, I don't
know what to say. I never expected a newcomer to
behave so handsomely."

"There's no need to say anything. If my uncle were still alive, I feel certain he would have approved."

The parson looked doubtful.

"Good day, Mr. Seymour."

"And to you, too, Miss Somerset." He walked away and shook his head while counting the coins a second time.

Sophie took the few remaining steps to the draper's shop. The bells tinkled when she closed the door and walked past the bolts of fabrics toward the counter. Seconds later the bells sounded again. The portly owner of the establishment barreled around the counter to take her order. She opened her mouth to speak but was interrupted by the person who had just entered.

"Pull down your finest wool and linen, sir," a tall stranger said, stepping forward. "Also, can you recommend the services of a tailor?" He turned and smiled at her. "Or perhaps there are no tailors to be found in this village?"

Just as she was about to give voice to her displeasure at the man's rudeness, Sophie found herself speechless before his fascinating appearance. Her mouth agape, she felt like a beached fish.

The outrageous gentleman sported a pale lavender waistcoat with an appliquéd design, a sea green coat with exaggerated cutaway styling and pinned back yellow lining, and while his shirt was a simple white, it had double rows of lace creeping from the cuffs and neck cloth. His skin tight breeches revealed the magnificence of every last inch of his physique.

The gentleman's Hessian boots featured an unusual white band with extra long tassels. Even among the priggish dandies in London, this gentleman must appear the veriest peacock.

Despite Sophie's considerable height, he dwarfed her by comparison. She drew herself up to her most imposing posture and tapped him on the arm.

"Excuse me, sir, but I believe the draper was about to take *my* order."

The gentleman raised an ornate quizzing glass to one eye and looked down his aquiline nose at her.

What an absurd picture he presented, one eye magnified to the size of a barn owl's peeper. She stifled a giggle. His gaze traveled over her from the tip of her head to her poor excuse for footwear. Bored hauteur was clearly an expression he had perfected.

"Really?" he drawled with amusement evident in the slight upturn at the corners of his mouth. He bowed and swept his arm in an invitation for her to step in front of him. "Pray forgive me. Do proceed."

What had she done? Now she had to place her order with this giant dandy standing witness. How provoking. Sophie assembled her thoughts.

"As I was about to say, I'd like to place an order for a warm cloak and, and for"—a sudden rush of heat flooded her face—"pantaloons and other suitable clothes for *a lady* who will be going on fishing expeditions and the like."

Sophie had lost her nerve. She'd wanted to have the fabric purchased and measured at the establishment. But the presence of the fancy gentleman next to her had overwhelmed her.

The draper tried to hide a smile but was unsuccessful. "And who would this lady be, miss?"

"Miss Somerset, lately of Villa Belza."

"The niece o' the old duke?"

"The very one," she replied, looking at her nails. For some reason she just couldn't bring herself to admit she was the lady in question. She knew without glancing that the exceptionally tall man beside her would have an amused arch to one eyebrow. He probably knew her game. She sneaked a peek at his expression.

Oh, he knew all right.

"Sorry, miss, my lord"—the man nodded to the stranger—"our tailor won't return for 'nother fortnight. But I can send a message when he's come."

"Oh," Sophie said, with disappointment. "I see."

"Perhaps you could inform the lady that I'd be delighted to offer her a pair of pantaloons?" the gentleman drawled. He lowered his shoulder to look down at her. "I could deliver them myself, of course. Unless she'd prefer a personal fitting at the house where I'm staying—Hinton Arms."

He winked at her.

The draper coughed and wheezed in an effort to withhold his amusement.

Of all the presumptuous audacity. Oh, why hadn't she just said she was Miss Somerset from the start? This was awkward in the extreme. Best to retreat soonest.

"Thank you, sir. You're very kind," Sophie said, lying through her teeth. She dropped a small curtsy and hastened from the shop.

Now she was stuck. She hadn't even ordered the material. She would just have to come back another day and see if there was anyone else in the vicinity who could make up a pair of simple pantaloons and a thick, warm coat instead of the flimsy town shawls good for nothing but decoration of the décolleté.

Of one thing she was sure. She would never set one foot near that gentleman's house. Now what was the name of his residence? Holton Mews? Hilton Grove?

William watched the lady in question's lovely derriere swish through the door of the shop. The only delightful thing about the atrocious footwear and rag she wore was that it failed to hide her beautiful trim ankles.

"Well," William said, turning to the draper. "A pity to let that one escape."

"I daresay, my lord, the young miss who just left was indeed, Miss Somerset."

"I haven't the slightest doubt of it," William said, smiling. While she was dressed like the poorest servant, he was surprised she hadn't been snapped up by one of the penniless members of the *ton* in London despite her disastrous entrée into the beau monde. It was obvious her transgression had left her reputation beyond repair.

"A fine fortune that one will bring to the altar, I hear tell," said the draper in conspiratorial tones. *"Ten thousand a year."*

William blinked. Good Lord. The mystery of why a fortune hunter in London hadn't snagged her hand deepened. She must've been caught in flagrante delicto. Perhaps she was with child. He cleared his throat and in that instant his mind assembled a brilliant idea.

She could provide the answer.

His man down from London had indicated there wasn't much time if he meant to continue with his plan.

He tried to concentrate on the task before him. "Let us begin again, then. I require a complete outfitting. Show me your shirt linen to start."

"Very good, my lord." The man brought down three bolts of fabric from the shelves behind him and laid them on the wooden counter, shiny from years of use.

William indicated the bolt of choice and pushed away a card of lace with a look of disgust. "Let's have a look at the possibilities for waistcoats and coats, if you please."

The man examined his finery and pulled a bolt of peach-colored silk from the shelves behind him.

"For God's sake, man, haven't you anything more somber or dignified?"

The draper's eyebrows rose in confusion from William's foppish appearance.

He felt exasperation creeping under the high shirt points of his ridiculous collar. Honestly, what was Farquhar thinking to own shirts like these? He couldn't remember if he'd ever spent a more ridiculous morning. Choosing fabric, indeed. Where was that bloody valet of his anyway?

As if on cue, tinkling doorbells heralded Jack Farquhar's entrance. If it was possible, his valet wore an even more outrageous display of male splendor. Pale rose breeches with mother-of-pearl buttons at the knees met black riding boots of the finest calf polished to a mirror finish.

Farquhar's ostentatious waistcoat was an embarrassment to mankind. The deep rose and green harlequin pattern matched the lapels of Farquhar's burgundy coat.

But the *pièce de résistance* was Farquhar's hat: a dashing woodman's design much like what Robin Hood was said to have sported, notwithstanding the rose-colored peacock feather erupting from the back.

The draper's hands, in the midst of retrieving another bolt from the shelves, stopped in midair. He gulped and appeared flustered.

"Thank God you're here to relieve me from the tedium of all this. You know what I require, Farquhar. Have it all sent to Hinton Arms and arrange for a tailor from London."

"How delightful! And I see we're in a bit of a temper this morning," the valet replied, then looked at the draper. "Let us have a look at that marvelous peach silk before you return it to the shelves, sir."

"Farquhar . . ." William said in a dark warning tone. "If I see one brightly colored article—"

The valet interrupted. "Oh, all right. If you're going to be fusty about it."

"Look at it this way. If you arrange for all my needs to *my* specifications, I'll treat you to a peach waistcoat."

"How divine. I love presents."

"I'll leave you to this then. I'm to the cobbler now."

"Oh, do bring back a bit of hide for Mrs. Tickle." Farquhar paused. "Please?"

"I'll not spend an instant on that good-for-nothing hound of yours. You go too far."

William turned to face the draper who looked thunderstruck by the exchange. The backcountry shopkeep had obviously never, in all his years, seen the likes of someone like Farquhar, a debonair dandy of the first order.

Indeed, Farquhar passed all boundaries of acceptable behavior and dress for a valet—or for any town fop for that matter. But his loyalty and honesty had surpassed all standards. Why, Will owed his very life to the man and vice versa. The war years might have been the start of their acquaintance and mutual admiration, but the months after had only strengthened their reliance on one another to hold close their secrets.

William turned to depart. But not before watching his valet rub his hands together in anticipation and ask to see the peach silk again. William shook his head. If Jack was not the finest valet in all of Christendom, and an excellent foil in their former spy games . . .

Chapter Three

Sophie nervously tapped the cream-colored velum card on her lap. She looked at it again.

> *The Misses Anna and Felicia Mornington request the pleasure of the company of Miss Somerset and Miss Owen for dinner Wednesday next, five o'clock.*

Oh dear. When she'd left London, Sophie had hoped she was through with dressing up and primping. She loathed the anxiety surrounding formal social occasions.

She would prefer spending an afternoon walking for miles along the beach or seeking out the two shepherds and the large flock of sheep on her uncle's vast estate.

There was nothing to be done. She must accept the invitation otherwise the talk about her in Burnham-by-the-Sea would include the term "hermit" instead of "eccentric," which she'd overheard below stairs early one morning. While she might not have appeared to care what others thought, there were times she was deeply hurt by the cool reception of the people in the area.

At least Mari would be happy about the invitation, Sophie thought while she composed a reply. Perhaps this would help her avoid her cousin's nightly harangue on her future state of poverty should the inheritance slip through Sophie's fingers.

Miss Somerset was proving to be an amusing diversion during the otherwise unimaginably dull visit in Bump-in-the-Sticks, William's new appellation for this loathsome, mucky corner of England.

He smiled inwardly. When she entered Mornington's formal salon, the look of horror on her face was beyond price. He'd never seen such an expression directed toward him. The gray-green fire in her almond-shaped eyes was as intriguing as he remembered. And she possessed the most exquisite creamy complexion with natural rosy cheeks, so unlike the painted ladies in town. Her decided chin spoke of intelligence and defiance.

If he was honest, her features were hard to fully appreciate from this distance. She'd seated herself as far away from him as possible, using generations of Mornington antiques to obstruct his view of her charming profile.

Enforced celibacy made him long to tangle his fingers in her thick dark blond hair, some of which had escaped the strict coronet of braids she'd fashioned.

William shook his head. Since when had gauche country misses interested him? Charles's simpering sisters had driven him to madness.

"Miss Somerset, may I say again what pleasure you and Miss Owens have given me and my sisters by joining us for dinner tonight?" Charles Mornington asked.

William's friend looked in good form tonight,

cutting a proper figure despite his short stature and stout frame. It was a pity William had not been able to fit himself into any of Mornington's more conservative garments.

William looked down at the ridiculous ensemble Farquhar had forced on him this evening. It was the worst yet, involving a dark orange-colored satin coat, bottle green knee breeches and a mulberry waistcoat with heavy gray brocade. He felt like a bloody gourd.

"Oh yes, Miss Somerset, Felicia and I are delighted you have joined the neighborhood. There are no other ladies"—and here Lady Anna sniffed—"who are of our caliber in the neighborhood."

"Anna and I were just saying that until we learned Lord Will had arrived here, we were having a dreadful time tearing ourselves away from the amusements in town," Lady Felicia said and dissolved into a round of high-pitched giggles.

Mornington's two juvenile sisters had been doggedly tailing Will for a fortnight. It was a wonder that two girls, not long from the schoolroom, had learned the game of cat and mouse so quickly. As they sat primly on the blue settee, he could almost imagine claws beneath their long gloves.

It would have been an altogether different story if they had been available for a dalliance. William would have been able to endure their silly chatter and cattish behavior. Ah, indeed . . . sometimes two ladies fighting over him in a bedchamber could be quite, quite . . . Oh hell, and damnation. Surrendering to celibacy was not in his nature.

Mornington stood up to signal the dining hour and looked to Miss Somerset.

William could not stop himself from claiming her

hand before his host, leaving Mornington to lead in the Welsh country cousin.

"Miss Somerset, allow me to take you in to dinner, my dear."

She flushed, which showed to advantage the cream and gold hue of her shoulders against the white silk gown with an apricot sash. Oh, yes, indeed, she presented a tempting morsel.

She refused to meet his eye but rose from the chaise and began to walk with him toward the double doors.

"Miss Somerset, I believe decorum dictates you take my arm," William said softly.

She reluctantly placed her arm on his without looking at him.

The party of six crossed the hall to enter into the austere magnificence of the dining hall.

"I have been wondering if you have a twin sister, Miss Somerset," he said for her ears only.

"A twin sister? Of course not. I am an only child."

"Then I should warn you that there was a dowd at a shop in the village who said she would pass a message to you. She had a remarkable resemblance to you, my dear."

"I have no idea what you are talking about, my lord. But I would appreciate it if you would refrain from calling me your 'dear.' I am not." Miss Somerset released his arm and attempted to move to the other side of the dining table.

It was a shame what the gossipmongers of London had done to this girl. Her bruised pride and reputation made her prudish and unsure. Yet he was delighted to have found her. She would prove to be a little bit of a challenge, he was sure. But a recently fallen young spinster, along with the most definite allure ten thousand a year brought, was exactly what was called for to alleviate the dull, limited society here.

"Ma chérie," William said under his breath as he caught her arm. "You must allow me to seat you to my right as is proper."

She paused, then looked at his hand on her arm and spoke quietly. "Please release me, sir. I have had my fill of etiquette lessons, thank you."

William smiled and removed his hand. "Pardon me. No offense was intended."

Miss Somerset turned her attention to the table. Everyone else was seated. Her expression, when she realized he had outmaneuvered her by stalling, was delightful. She sent him a glance that could have melted a snowbank and stiffly sat in the chair beside him, assuming an uncompromising, rigid posture.

Mornington had placed Miss Owens to his right and his elder sister, Felicia, at the foot. Anna Mornington looked annoyed at finding herself between her sister and Miss Owens. Soon enough the younger sister engaged the attention of her tablemates with mindless banter.

"Miss Somerset," William asked in low tones, "may we dispense with your falsehoods at the draper's? For I wish to know if you have been successful in your pursuit of a pair of . . . well, a pair of pantaloons."

"I thank you for your interest, sir, however, it should be of no concern to you."

"Ah. Quite right. It's just that I feel compelled as a gentleman"—William arched an eyebrow—"to offer the services of a tailor down from London tomorrow."

"Thank you for this news, my lord. I'll arrange

for his services myself when I'm next in the village." She picked up the water goblet, and took a long swallow, giving him time to admire the long, slender line of her neck.

"I see I've not explained properly," William said. "I am afraid the tailor shall be housed here to take care of my extensive needs."

She glanced at him with surprise. It was obvious she thought him a hopeless dandy—only concerned with maintaining the first blaze of fashion. But, perhaps, this would play to his advantage given her skittish nature and distaste of fortune hunters.

"But I suppose I could spare him part of the morning if—"

Like a fish grabbing the bait, she reached. "If what?"

"If you would return *here* for the fitting." He unfolded his napkin and placed it on his lap with elegant gestures. "Alas, while I'm most willing to lend the talents of my tailor to a desperate female, I cannot spare him above a half hour. You may consider it penance for your prior sin of dishonesty."

Her cheeks became pink, her muted green eyes sparked, and her bosom, ah, well, it was most becoming when she took a deep breath in indignation, as she did now.

"A desperate female? Outrageous. But, then you are not content unless you are just so. I see your methods. But"—she smiled—"I'll not give you the pleasure of an argument. I accept your offer and shall return here tomorrow morning to meet your tailor, which you *so kindly* offered for precisely one half hour."

Miss Anna Mornington intruded in their exchange. "I would like a share in your conversation, if you please," she insisted petulantly. "The seating tonight is very inconvenient. Miss Somerset, do tell us the sorts of amusements you favor. We simply must organize some diversions or Felicia and I will go mad being away from London in the middle of the Season."

"Well, actually, I enjoy walking. This area has an extraordinary stark beauty to it, especially the paths along the shoreline."

Mornington's sister took on a peevish expression. "I was hoping you might choose to have a dinner and some dancing one of these evenings. It has been ages since we have been to the villa. Not since before Mama's and the duke and duchess's deaths."

"Anna, that was ill done of you," said Mornington. "Now you have put Miss Somerset in the uncomfortable position of feeling obligated to abide by your wishes."

Fortune was smiling on him today, thought William. All eyes focused on Miss Somerset.

"No, no, that's quite all right, Mr. Mornington. I would be delighted to devise an evening at Villa Belza," Miss Somerset said. "I am afraid it is long overdue."

"My cousin was saying just yesterday, when we received your kind invitation"—Miss Mari Owens cleared her throat—"that she *longed* for entertainments of that sort too."

The petite Welsh cousin was a skilled liar if he was forced to hazard a guess. Mornington had not seemed able to tear his eyes away from the dark beauty all evening. Now William would not even be able to count on Mornington for rational conversation. Indeed, his friend wore the same lovesick mooncalf expression his sisters wore on Will's behalf. William would have to converse with Miss Somerset then, ah, but he would really rather taste the delicacies of her . . .

"Shall we say Saturday, next? My cousin and I would be honored if all of you would join us for dinner and perhaps some music, if any of you play," said Miss Somerset, hiding her reluctance.

"Oh, how wonderful," exclaimed Miss Anna Mornington, clapping her hands together. "Felicia and I would be pleased to perform for you."

Oh dear God, thought William, not another evening of screeching and sonatas missing a number of notes.

Suddenly, the familiar sound of a scrambling dog whose nails were failing to catch on hard flooring preceded the appearance of a sausagelike dab of tan and black. An oath not fit for the polite world escaped a nearby servant's lips when the creature dodged the man's hands and leapt into William's lap.

Mrs. Tickle carried a shoe between her teeth, a newly tooled calf shoe, *his shoe*. She dropped it in his lap, panted and looked up for approval.

The high-pitched garble of Jack Farquhar in the hall followed before the man himself made an appearance. Farquhar, bless his heart, was all done up in his most elegant finery for his evening off. Varying shades of pistachio were being put to the test tonight. But no, a hint of yellow and white peeked above and below the satin coat proving that yellow polka dots could compete admirably with vivid green.

"Oh, Mr. Mornington, ladies, sir," said Farquhar bowing as low as his stiff shirt points would allow. "I say, sorry to intrude."

"Farquhar," William said slowly, with an edge.

"Oh yes, of course. Mustn't interrupt the fine ladies and gentlemen. Where is that sorry dog of mine? Oh, there you are sweetheart." Jack Farquhar spied his pug and came around. "There, there, you mustn't make such a fuss when deprived of the new bit of hide"—the valet glared at William—"*someone* forgot to bring you."

William passed the dog and mauled shoe to his valet.

"I will require a word with you later, Farquhar."

"Oui, monseigneur." The valet adopted his most formal stance and clicked his heels while bowing.

Farquhar departed while cooing silly nothings in his pet's ear, but not before everyone noticed him slipping William's shoe back to Mrs. Tickle for the pug's further enjoyment. The door closed shut.

"I'm all amazement by the long leash you allow your man," Mornington said, recovering from shock.

"Yes, well, I suppose I tolerate it because he allows my leash to be equally long." William would never forget the number of times he had been unable to pay Farquhar during the last year and the man's unquestioning loyalty and bravery.

William turned to see Miss Somerset on the verge of bursting with laughter. Tears filled her eyes and a delicate napkin covered her mouth.

"You find this amusing, Miss Somerset."

"How could one not?" she said with laughter.

Well, at least Farquhar had accomplished what he had not. She was finally at ease and looking as if she was enjoying herself. And it was a sight to behold, merriment in her eyes and a charmingly pretty smile.

William turned to see the ever-present reverent expressions on Mornington's silly sisters. It was not every day he encountered a female unwilling to preen and flirt with him. Miss Somerset obviously mistook him for a harmless dandy.

It was insulting.

It was delightfully amusing.

It presented an irresistible challenge and sparked a devilish idea for bringing about an end to his fiscal woes, with the added benefit of providing amusement to his stay in this backwater village on the edge of nowhere.

The early morning of the following day, Sophie retraced the path of the evening before. There was certainly no harm in spending a half-hour's time in an upstairs chamber of Hinton Arms, accompanied by her maid, Mademoiselle Karine. The tailor would not dare ask her to undress. He would simply measure her waist and the length to the floor, and she would ask him to estimate the roundness of her lower limbs.

The imposing thirteenth century stone manor house, adorned with elegant chimneys and carved parapets, came into view. A newly constructed Palladian bridge with clusters of jonquils surrounding the bases provided an elegant passageway over a narrow section of lake, which fronted the house. Sophie smiled as she thought what Aunt Rutledge's opinion would be of the idea of Sophie having a pair of pantaloons made to go fishing. London felt wonderfully far away, indeed.

Of one thing she was certain. She had nothing to fear from Lord William, especially this early in the morning. He was a do-nothing bit of frippery who would surely have *tonnish*, slug-a-bed tendencies. Truly, the man cared for nothing more than lavish displays of colorful silks, rivaling the rainbow. And his curious man, Mr. Farquhar, was a strange popinjay of awe-inspiring proportions.

The Misses Mornington had claimed he was Lord William's valet, but certainly this could not be so. What man of the serving class would be allowed such freedom of dress and behavior? Lord William seemed to be on the most intimate of terms with his employee.

Yet there was something, that certain something, Sophie could not quite put her finger on that made her pause. Perhaps it was the something in Lord William's dark, flashing eyes that matched his longish dark brown hair. The intelligence she was sure she had glimpsed in his expression was at odds with the dimples she had caught sight of once. But they looked so seductive on his smooth, tanned cheeks that set off his white teeth when he chose to reveal them.

Sophie shook her head. This was ridiculous.

And then there was the matter of his hands. She had not failed to notice the calluses on his palms when he had removed his gloves prior to dinner. They were hands that did not match his aristocratic airs, mien and clothes.

They reminded Sophie of her father's hands—strong, purposeful and capable. She remembered her father's large palmed hand stroking her hair as she sat in his lap by the fire after they had spent a fruitful day on the sea, in the pastures or ministering to the needs of the parish.

She swallowed her sadness and mentally shook herself. At least she was not as homesick in Burnham-by-the-Sea as she had been in London. She could essentially live the same sort of life here as she had had in Wales albeit in more opulence.

Sophie negotiated the gray marble steps to the

landing. There was no sign of activity. Perhaps she *had* come a mite early. Karine had appeared half-asleep, trudging silently one step behind her mistress the entire way. Her French maid seemed to have little interest in invigorating excursions of any type, seeming to prefer consuming the latest *on-dits* and a hot pot of chocolate before a fire more than anything else. Truth be told, Sophie was a bit intimidated with the petite, calculating woman.

"Do you think we are too early, then, Karine?" Sophie said, lifting the knocker and letting it fall.

"Yes," Karine said with her usual Gallic shrug. "But then, it would have been too early if you had waited two hours from now." The maid yawned.

Sophie wondered if she would ever be able to control her maid's outlandish tongue. If it wasn't that her aunt had insisted the maid had more talent than . . .

The heavy oak door swung open and within moments she was being ushered to the tailor's apartment by a young footman. Karine disappeared in the direction of the servants' back stairs, chattering with another maid who appeared. Sophie passed a breathtaking picture gallery containing floor-to-ceiling portraits of Mornington ancestors. She and the footman padded along several corridors and more stairs until he stopped in front of an ornate door at the end of a long hallway.

He knocked and turned to Sophie. "This be where the tailor has set out his things, miss. I'll leave you here, then." He bowed and quickly walked away.

Sophie heard a distinctly masculine voice from within, which seemed to suggest that she should enter. She pushed down the brass handle and opened the door.

Good Lord. She inhaled sharply.

Sophie snapped out of shock, closed the door abruptly and looked around to see if anyone had observed the spectacle.

She licked her lips and tried to still her quaking limbs. Heart pounding, she turned and fled down the endless passageway.

Lord William had been standing before her *in the altogether,* just come from his bath. He had been toweling his dark hair, leaving all the world to see his towering, muscled magnificence in the golden sunlight streaming in through the window beyond.

She had never seen anything like him. Indeed, the fishermen and townspeople of Porthcall did not seem to be of the same species!

Sophie stopped at the end of the corridor and gripped the corner, the directions back to the front hall completely forgotten. She closed her eyes but could not escape her mind's vision of the man who so perfectly matched her idea of Adonis.

Sophie's gaze had been instantly drawn to his, his . . . well, to the very part of him that indicated his desire. That part of his anatomy had looked nothing like the Greek marble statue she had seen in the foyer at one of the grander London townhouse balls she had attended. A fig leaf, no, two fig leaves would not have been large enough to cover . . . Her breath finally seemed to desert her in one long exhale.

He had turned to notice her and a slow smile had spread across his face, revealing the wicked dimples. He had thrown back his head and laughed.

Sophie was about to flee, despite her uncertainty of the correct path back to the main hall, when she heard from behind her a deep baritone voice laced with the slightest hint of a French accent.

"*Chérie,* this is delightful. Do come back. I was

just thinking about you," Lord William called out, chuckling. "Although I did not think my wishes would be granted so quickly."

Sophie turned to see Lord William standing in the hallway only slightly more decent. He had donned a white lawn shirt, which just covered his obvious masculinity. Sophie found she could not draw her eyes away from his chest, as the fabric was rendered invisible in some places from his still wet body.

She swallowed. "Excuse me. I—I'm sorry to have intruded," Sophie said, averting her eyes finally. "I was told your tailor was here. I must leave."

She turned and began to retrace her steps toward the main stair but his words stilled her steps.

"*Chérie,* come back or I'll be forced to come after you in this, ah, state of undress."

He wouldn't dare. She lifted her chin in defiance.

His eyes twinkled and he walked toward her. "My tailor is waiting for you. He just stepped away for a moment while I finished my bath," he replied, making a motion with his arms to urge her to precede him back to the room. "You may come in now."

"I think not. I'll return to the lower salon until your tailor will see to my needs." Her gaze remained glued to the carpet.

"Are you afraid?" he asked, tugging on a blue dressing gown she just now noticed he had carried over his arm. His dark eyes dipped to her line of vision. "I promise you I'm modest now, even by England's more repressive standards."

Sophie sighed. She was not at all sure she would be able to find her way back without getting lost. "And where is Mr. Farquhar?"

"Gone to prepare the rest of my morning toilette," Lord William said, releasing her hand to rub his fingers over his morning shadow of whiskers.

"I'm sure he has," Sophie said under her breath.

"What did you say, *chérie*?"

"Nothing. Nothing at all. Oh, this is very awkward."

"It doesn't have to be," he said, winking. "Come now, we can't have you standing about in the hallway. Do come in. I promise not to bite." Lord William took her hand gently and encouraged her back down the hallway and over the threshold, keeping the glimmer in his dark eyes.

"I'm not intimidated by you, Lord William. I assure you I am not."

"All the better. I've never been able to tolerate shrinking violets."

"There's no reason for me to fear you, given your inclinations."

He looked as if he would burst out laughing. Instead he smothered a smile and attempted a poor imitation of contriteness. "Then we understand each other, *chérie*. It will make it so much less tiresome if I do not have to explain everything to you."

He raked his longish wet hair back from his face, oozing charm from every pore. "We are agreed then that I'm a perfectly harmless gentleman. I'm also a generous man, and as such, I invite you to go first. The tailor is just through the passage in the adjoining chamber." He cupped her chin in his hand. "I may be depraved, *chérie,* but I will not let it be said that I'm not considerate of a lady's sensibilities."

"Please stop calling me that. I'm not your *chérie*."

He took one step closer to her. *"Non?"*

"Non!" And before she could stop herself, she blurted out, "I know your game."

"Really? Pray tell, what is it?"

She did not have the nerve to tell him her thoughts concerning Mr. Farquhar, especially when his handsome frame towered over her and his eyes glowed with mischief.

"But I must be allowed to call someone *'chérie.'* Life will be unimaginably dull if I cannot have a *female friend* who understands me." Lord William bowed and looked up with a devastating smile. "You slay my heart, Miss Somerset. I suppose I'll be forced to turn my attentions to the Mornington sisters for feminine camaraderie. Do you think they'll agree to endure the alarming designation?"

She felt unaccountably irritated by the idea. And annoyed more so with herself and the way her stomach churned every time she looked into his dark eyes. She hated being such a fool.

A knock sounded on the half-closed door separating the two chambers. The shiny pate of a small man peered around the doorframe. "Excuse me, my lord. Shall I await— Oh, I do beg your pardon, miss," he said, seeing Sophie and bobbing quickly.

"That's quite all right," Lord William said. "Miss Somerset was just on her way in." He looked down at her as the little man disappeared. "I've something I'd like to discuss further with you, *chér—* Miss Somerset. Would you allow me to escort you to Villa Belza after your fitting?"

"I'm shocked, sir," she replied, trying to appear lighthearted. "I had rather thought your appointment with the tailor would take precedence over taking the air with a female. But, yes, you may escort me."

He laughed and brought her hand to his beautiful, full lips. "I shall await you with impatience then, *Miss Somerset.*"

Sophie could not control the slight frisson of excitement that flowed from her hand to her heart. He looked up at her, his lips now an inch from her glove, and gently turned her hand in his own to press a kiss on the sensitive flesh of her wrist.

Oh, he was wicked, indeed. It was all so confusing, she thought as she walked into the fitting room.

As the tailor went about his work, Sophie smiled. She forced herself to acknowledge that she rather liked the idea of continuing their conversation despite the guilt she felt, knowing her father would never have approved of deepening an acquaintance with a man of such dubious character. But, she really had nothing to fear from him, considering his preferences. She had more to fear, if she was honest, with her own reactions toward him. He was the handsomest man she had ever seen. She would have to take care not to make a cake of herself.

At least, he had not shown any indications of being a fortune hunter like Lord Coddington. His array of clothes alone had most likely cost a small fortune. And she hazarded that gentlemen such as he never married.

Lord William had only ever exhibited an inclination toward one particular transgression. And given that Sophie was a vicar's daughter, and had witnessed some of the basest aspects of human nature while attending to her deceased father's parishioners, she did not fear vice as she had learned everyone was a sinner in the eyes of the Lord. And it seemed that this particular gentleman's failing didn't hurt anyone except himself, which was a lesser offense according to her father.

*   *   *

Miss Somerset's delightful maid had provided William the ideal opportunity for a delicate conversation. During the long walk back to the lady's villa, the maid's fragile slippers had given way to the abuses of a dirty, pebble-strewn country lane.

William had hailed a passing neighbor's dogcart and enlisted the man's aid in transporting the girl back to her mistress's residence. He had ignored the maid's schemes to trap him into carrying her back to the villa. If Miss Somerset had understood the sexual nature of her saucy servant's flirtatious suggestions in French, the maid would have been sacked in a thrice. As it was, William was hard put not to take the girl up on her offer. She was a petite, fetching Frenchwoman despite her overpowering perfume and bold suggestions.

But Mr. Derby's demands took precedence. If William did not secure the necessary funds soon, all would be lost.

Now he was left with a brief half hour to ensnare his prey with his sinful proposal. It could work. It was the only plan he had, given Miss Somerset's apparent dislike of fortune hunters and her confusion over his character. Yes, it might well work after all was said and done.

"Miss Somerset, I'm hoping you will allow me the freedom of speaking plainly."

"I daresay I've little say in the matter, sir."

"Well, since you've already seen me without a stitch"—he stopped upon seeing her shocked expression. "Ahem, I thought you wouldn't mind if we dispense with trivial talk such as the weather?"

"The weather can provide for stimulating conversation at times, my lord. This might just be the exact topic we should choose."

"My dear Miss Somerset, I'm here to offer you

my help. I've heard of your misfortunes in London—of not being able to attract an eligible parti—but let's speak no more of the pack of fools inhabiting London these days." He dared not look at her face lest he lose his nerve. He rushed on. "I would like to propose to teach you the art of finding and attracting a husband."

She had stopped walking. He retraced two steps to rejoin her.

"Well, I suppose I should be surprised and insulted by your unusual proposal. But I find I cannot be either." She glanced the length of his physique. "I'm very sure *you* could teach me to attract a gentleman—an art you have evidently honed to perfection. Attracting gentlemen, I mean."

She was steadier than he would have guessed.

"However, there's a flaw in your plan," she continued.

"A flaw?"

"Yes," she said, pulling a pale blue shawl more tightly about her shoulders. "I've no interest in securing a titled fortune hunter for a husband. I'm returning to Wales."

"Ah, I see. You have a love match all pat and secure, waiting for you in your quaint little village in Wales?"

"Porthcall."

"Ah, in Porthcall, then?"

"No, I do not."

He dipped his head to get a better view of her expression. Her eyes were curiously composed. At least she wasn't blushing and turning missish on him. "Then you've convinced the relative who shall parcel out the inheritance that you're worthy without benefit of a husband?"

"You know a lot about my affairs, Lord William."

"As do you about my own, Miss Somerset."

"Touché, sir. We are both of us in uncomfortable situations."

"Yes, my dear—uh, Miss Somerset. But you're in a position to acquire what you ought to have, and I can help you."

"I thank you, but it is unnecessary. I have taken my decision and it shall stand."

"You're actually going to allow ten thousand pounds a year to slip from your grasp?" He tried to make his tone sound neutral.

"No. It is actually more like fifteen thousand a year."

William closed his eyes in shock. *Good God.*

"But my Aunt Rutledge thought it would be better if we didn't reveal that high a sum straightaway. She thought I'd be able to attract the right sort dangling just ten." She looked away. "However, my awkward and vulgar behavior, I am told, took care of squelching any possible hope of connections to the *ton*."

"You are wrong, my dear." He took hold of her chin gently and drew her gaze back to his. "I'm certain, no matter how great your transgressions, you could secure a comfortable marriage easily, with a bit of coaching from me, behind the scenes, so to speak."

"I told you, I have decided to return to Wales. I have no need of a husband."

"Well, perhaps you are right. You probably couldn't attract a flea for a spouse given your reputation at this moment in time."

She puffed up in indignation. "I could say the same to you, sir."

Ah, she was falling right into his plan. "Perhaps. Yet, perhaps not. Care to wager on it?"

"What? On your ability to be attracted to a proper lady and actually wed her versus my ability to attract and wed a lord?" She began to laugh in earnest.

Well. It was insulting. Did she really think he wouldn't have his pick of a thousand ladies? It was a first.

"Yes, that is precisely what I had in mind, Miss Somerset. In shall we say, three months' time? And by the by, I accept your challenge."

"Accept my challenge? I did not—" she said before he interrupted.

"Oh, yes, you did. But I've forgotten. You are Welsh and the Welsh are known for reneging on challenges."

She was well and truly hooked if the look on her face was any indication. She was a gambler at heart.

"Well, I shall prove you wrong, sir."

"Now we must discuss the terms, *chérie*."

"The terms?"

She seemed to have forgotten her prior dislike of the endearment. "Yes, what each of us would gain from this understanding. I daresay I shouldn't have to give you a farthing if you're successful before me, given the promise of fifteen thousand a year."

She had a disturbing gleam in her eye. "Oh, you would get off too easily, my lord. Let us say that you would have to walk clear around Hyde Park during the social hour dressed in an ensemble I should pick out for you."

William threw back his head and laughed. "No doubt it involves some hideous Welsh fisherman's rags? Oh, you are very good, mademoiselle. Very good indeed," he said, smiling. "But now it is my turn. I fear I must be equally devious. If I'm able to find a *female* I would be willing to actually marry"—and here he shuddered theatrically—"thereby giving up my current lifestyle, and if she should accept my proposal, you would be required to—to burn all those disgusting peasant rags you own, and wear only proper, pretty gowns to Farquhar's specifications. And no pantaloons, ever."

"What?" She looked distressed.

"Well, we must make it worth the effort. And furthermore, each much approve the other's choice of spouse," William said. "As I am a gentleman," he said, taking her arm and wrapping it within his own before continuing toward the villa, "I feel it only sporting if we agree to assist or teach each other in the provocative arts of securing a partner."

"I'm not at all sure I will approve of your ways."

"Yes, but you must try to be unprejudiced. As you said, I'm familiar with what gentlemen are looking for."

She gurgled with laughter. "Oh, all right. But what if we both fail in this ridiculous endeavor? I for one find it a distinct possibility." She was looking him over from the tip of Farquhar's ridiculous new hat to the overly tight breeches in crimson.

"I never fail, mademoiselle."

"I see," she said, suppressing a smile.

"It is agreed then. Now regarding the lessons. I propose the first shall begin tomorrow, in secret. It seems you favor taking the air along the seashore. I shall inadvertently be strolling along the same path as you tomorrow, precisely at the ungodly early hour of ten o'clock."

"And what will the lesson entail?"

"Let's start alphabetically, *chérie*, shall we? Let's see. . . . A for Attitude, B for Behavior and let us

say also"—he eyed her primly restrained breasts—
"Bosoms and how they should be displayed to their
best advantage." He fully expected her to strike
him for that indiscretion but it seemed he couldn't
shock her. She might have turned an alarming beet
red in embarrassment, but she apparently viewed
him as an intimate friend—like a sister.

"All right, my lord. And I shall teach you about
C, D, and E—Character, Distaste for dandies, and
the Error of your ways—all of which my father
taught me well."

At least she recovered from embarrassment rapidly. She now wore the gleefully happy expression
he enjoyed teasing to full blossom.

"Ah, I see. You hope to truly reform me then,
chérie."

"Indeed, my upbringing demands it. Shall we
begin? Or do you need time to contemplate the
course of our mutual education?"

Chapter Four

"*W*hy would I need to know where you're going so early in the morning?" Farquhar brushed the shoulders and back of the light gray coat adorning William. The valet peered around to look at Will's reflection in the cheval glass. "It's not my place to be wondering that sort of thing, is it now? Not even when you wouldn't rise this early for a meeting with royalty." Farquhar sniffed.

"Oh, I don't know." William held back a grin. "Perhaps you are right about the Prince Regent. The man is a dead bore. But, I suppose I would rise to see the queen at this unholy hour—but so far, I've been fortunate. She rises later than I."

"Well, I for one am glad those escapades"—Farquhar lifted his eyebrows as high as possible—"are long over. I am still having nightmares over those trysts. I was sure we'd be tossed out of the country—made to swim the Channel, despite everything we did for the Crown."

"As I remember, you have nothing to complain about. You won more bets below stairs than any gentleman at White's."

"And how else was I to eat?" Farquhar took a deep breath to launch into his favorite topic. "What with the many long years of sorry pay from British intelligence for risking our bloody necks, and the *inconsistent* manner I am currently compensated . . ."

"Martyrdom never suited you."

"Well." Farquhar's face puckered. "I see we are evading questions this morning."

"Do you have a fan, dear boy?" William said, turning from the glass. At least he had found a coat of Farquhar's that was a touch more conservative. The white pantaloons were another story. They were so tight they bordered on the obscene.

"A fan? Certainly." Farquhar looked delighted by the proposition of William stretching his personal wardrobe to the limits. On the way to retrieve the article, Farquhar stopped in midstride. "What, pray tell, are you going to do with a fan at nine o'clock in the morning?"

Knowledge dawned.

"Ah. So we have a little assignation planned? With a certain female. A lady, I presume, with the care you have taken this morning. And is my fan to be a gift? I'm not at all sure I can part with it. It was painted by a celebrated artist and is worth—"

"Just give me the fan, Jack. I shall return it to you before noon," William interrupted the endless stream of his valet's words.

"Touchy, aren't we?"

Farquhar disappeared for a moment and returned carrying two fans of differing sizes. "Now you must take great c—"

"Thank you," William said, taking both fans from Farquhar in midsentence.

"You promised there would be no more running and hiding." Farquhar attached a tiny white rosebud to William's lapel and looked him square in the face. "Just tell me you are not planning on seducing those silly Mornington chits. Even though I can't abide their brother, I've no desire to go willy-nilly about the country again so soon. And Lord knows I'd have to ask for references and my last pay if I had to face the sight of one of those females in your bed for the rest of my life."

"Your observations never fail to amuse. And you know I haven't a farthing to pay you for the last quarter. So I daresay I'll have to allow other, more"—he scratched his chin—"charitable gentlemen the honor of courting the Misses Mornington."

"Then—"

"Then, nothing, *mon vieux*. I am out to take the air."

"The air? You? Take the air at ten o'clock?"

William murmured his assent.

"Ah, then it must be the Welsh female. At least she has tolerable teeth and knows when to stop clacking them."

William laughed. "So she does."

"Well, don't forget Mr. Derby will be coming to see you this afternoon along with the architect. They cannot be put off much longer."

"That is why I look the veritable bridegroom, dear boy," William said.

Jack Farquhar stopped brushing the lint from the back of William's coat. "Far be it from me to give you my opinion," he huffed. "Besides, feelings of guilt have never been your forte."

Sophie knew she was being foolish. She had taken extraordinary care in her dress on this glorious blue-sky morning. It was something she had not cared to do since leaving London's elegant townhouses.

She bounded down the steep descent of the footpath to the narrow strip of sand below. Her white silk gown with gold braiding billowed out behind her as a gust of wind played havoc with her carefully coiffed curls.

She had even allowed Karine to squeeze her into the horrid contraption meant to flatten and minimize her top-heavy physique. Her maid seemed to take delight in torturing her. It wasn't as tight as it had been during the last, almost fatal, interview with Lord Coddington, but still it made breathing difficult. She endured it because Lord William had said they would discuss her bosom—of all the audacious topics. Why, in all her years she had never heard a gentleman utter that word. Sophie pulled up the edge of the gown's low band of silk to conceal herself more.

"Miss Somerset, delighted to see you." Lord William pushed away from a tall rock and handed her down from the small berm of sand above the beach. "I wondered if you would renege on our agreement."

"Of course not. I'm curious to hear your advice, my lord," Sophie said. "It is certain to be less tedious than Aunt Rutledge's lessons on becoming a lady."

He bowed his head slightly and winked at her. "If I cannot entertain you, how can I hope to educate?"

·She placed her hand on his broad forearm and for the first time in her life Sophie felt petite and almost feminine. He was so very tall and large in the shoulders. His gray coat seemed ready to burst at the seams. And his pantaloons. How ever did he get them on? What sort of gentleman wore such tight-fitting white pantaloons, which outlined . . . She averted her gaze.

This sort of gentleman.

"So you plan to teach me about 'attitude' while we walk?"

"I believe we can canvas all of the topics by the time we reach the Berrow, which if I remember correctly, is not more than two miles from here. And then you shall have the return to teach me your tricks." He smiled with just a twinge of wickedness.

The sun shone brightly, its rays bounced off the wavelets. A dozen small seagulls screeched, dipping and soaring in the stiff breeze above the shallow hollows of the tufts of sea grasses.

Out of the corner of her eye, Sophie saw Lord Will pull two fans out of his coat. The first, made of painted ivory and black lace, he handed to her. With a refined, practiced gesture, he opened the other, a mask fan on a delicate bone monture. He peered through the eyeholes and winked at her.

Sophie smiled. "What is this?"

"Attitude, *ma chérie*. Nothing conveys self-assuredness and sly innuendo as well as a fan used properly." He wafted the air with a haughty feminine elegance.

Sophie stopped and laughed until tears coursed down her face.

"I do beg your pardon," William said dryly. "To begin, holding a fan in your left hand, like this, indicates that you would like to make the other party's acquaintance. This is especially useful when you want to bypass about twenty fusty relatives in the courtship process."

"Of course, how dandy." She began to laugh again.

"Do be serious," he said, closing the fan with a snap and poking Sophie in the ribs.

"Ouch!"

"That's not at all the response you would want from a gentleman."

"Whatever do you mean?"

"Poking means, 'I like you. Pay attention to me.' "

"Oh, I see."

"Now you try," Will said.

Sophie held the fan in her right hand and half opened it in front of her face.

"No, no, no. Half opened with the right hand in front of the face indicates 'I don't like you, I love another.' "

Sophie shook her head and grinned. "No wonder I scared them all away in droves."

Will used his closed fan to gently brush a strand of curls that had fallen from her coiffure.

"And I suppose that meant something?"

Will smiled and Sophie was dazzled anew by his handsome features.

"You learn quickly, *chérie*. It means 'Do not forget me.' "

She looked up into his laughing eyes. "Don't worry. I shan't."

Oh dear, God, what was she saying to him? It was those warm brown eyes of his that always made it hard to think properly. She swallowed and tried to regain her composure.

"If that is the case in this mock seduction then you must fan your face quickly, indicating your passion for me," he said slyly, coming around more fully to face her. He stilled her fan with his hand and closed it. "And now, if you wish to encourage an honorable gentleman's intentions, you would tap the handle on his lips." William reversed the fan's ends and returned it to her hands.

Gently, ever so gently, Sophie held her breath and brushed the handle on Will's full, bronzed lips.

He arched one brow and glanced at her mouth.

Sophie licked her dry lips and couldn't breathe.

"Ah. So we proceed to the next lesson—kissing," he whispered.

Sophie dropped her gaze. "I thought it was . . . uh . . . bodices."

"Bosoms, *ma chérie*. Yes, kissing and the other go nicely together, indeed." He led her over to the relative seclusion of a rock ledge.

"I really don't think I need any lessons in either, my lord." She was unable to meet his gaze.

"Ah, but you do, my dear. I guarantee the ladies *and gentlemen* of London have refined techniques. And since you cannot return to London and reassume the hunt for a husband using the innocent virgin method"—and here he batted his eyelashes and tittered behind his fan—"you must become thoroughly practiced in the arts of a flirtatious coquette."

She wasn't at all sure she had the nerve to actually kiss him. He was far too handsome, far too uninterested in her. She loathed the idea of making a fool of herself.

"Then," he continued, "you'll drive the gentlemen all wild with longing and you'll have your choice of all the hopefuls. And who better to show you than me? For I'm perfectly harmless, by your own words, am I not?" William lifted her chin with his large hand. "And perhaps," he said, rolling his eyes, "you'll tempt me to throw off the shackles of my *unnatural nature*."

"All right," she said quietly, unexpectedly. It wasn't what she'd meant to say. It was just that the picture he'd presented, that of all the Lord Codfishes of London on their knees and begging for her hand with true desire in their eyes, tantalized her.

Her hand slowly moved the handle of the fan over the dark flesh of his lips.

She looked up at him with huge trusting eyes.

He almost felt a twinge of guilt. Almost. He shook himself. This was ridiculous. It was not as if she was a virgin. The London papers had been most explicit in her fallen status. He hardened his resolve when her lips glistened invitingly in the sunshine.

He lowered his face to hers and paused for just the slightest moment. Pausing before a kiss heightened desire and gave the illusion he cared enough to give her a last chance to cry off. For some confounded reason he found it difficult to proceed.

The lightest touch of cool fingertips swept across his cheek, like an innocent dove fluttering against him. He shuddered and closed his eyes.

All at once, her tender lips brushed a kiss on his cheek.

He angled his mouth toward hers and returned the kiss, barely resting on the softness he found nestled there. He resisted the urge to part his lips and crush her to him. William breathed deeply and pushed slightly away.

"Ah yes, the innocent kiss. *Ma chérie,* I think you've mastered that one quite well," William whispered, looking down at the dazed sweetness of her face.

He tried to reassemble his thoughts and his campaign. "Let's proceed to the flirtatious kiss, then, shall we? One you must master if you intend to slay the heart of a suitable gentleman."

"I don't know if this is really necces—"

He lowered his head and captured her lips once again, swallowing the rest of her words all at once. For long moments he teased the seam of her lips with his tongue, urging her to open to him. Her light breath on his cheek aroused him and it took every ounce of self-control not to gather her up in his arms. Instead, he cupped her face with his hands and teased the tendrils of hair that had come loose in the slight breeze.

He longed to touch her breasts. Her shape fascinated him. He'd seen her tiny waist silhouetted in the sunlight. And her tall carriage supported the most impressive display of femininity he'd ever beheld, despite the rigid armor she sported.

With a slowness meant to torment him, he moved his hands to her waist and gently slid his hands up the sides of her body. He inhaled deeply her rose scent and placed his hands on the sensitive area below her breasts.

A sheet of hardened metal—or something like hardened metal—greeted his hand. This was no simple corset. He'd never felt anything like it before.

Reluctantly, he broke off the kiss and rested his forehead against hers. "My dear, this, this article you're wearing is impossible. How can you even breathe?"

Before she could answer him, he nudged the edge of the silk bodice and found the strings of a bow holding an exceptionally wide tooled whalebone busk in place. He deftly untied the laces and pulled out the tortuous device in a fluid movement before she could stop him.

"My lord!" she exclaimed. "That was very wrong of you. Give it back!"

She had the most beautiful eyes. So easy to read

and openly honest. "No, I think not. We should send it off to London—where they're always looking for new forms of torture to coerce confessions."

His gamble worked. She couldn't hide the merriment in her expression.

"I sense it not only hampers your breathing, *chérie,* but will dampen the spirits of your most ardent admirers. You must never use this again, unless you have need of a chastity device," he added dryly.

"My aunt says I must wear it lest I appear too common. And I'm so tired of males looking at me with knowing glances. It's always been the case, even at twelve years old."

He shook his head. "*Chérie,* there are ladies who would gladly give their teeth to have your physique. You must stop covering yourself, and start taking pride in your, mmmm, assets."

"Well, I'll admit it's difficult to breathe with it. I know I should be mortified, but I feel ever so much better." Miss Somerset smiled timidly.

"No, no. You have exquisite teeth. You must smile more fully and raise your head to look down the end of your nose at us, the less fortunate members of the *ton*. That's it. Now we must practice the kiss again, and you must open your mouth this time."

"What?" She looked flustered. "Oh, this is ridiculous."

"Come, come, you almost had me thinking of petticoats and stockings instead of, of waistcoats and watch fobs. Let's try again." He stifled his smile and kissed her again. God help him if she obeyed his instructions.

She did.

The lapping of waves drummed out of his head

as the heat of the blood in his veins pounded his temples. She was utterly delicious, all sweet femininity and boundless honest charm. Unconsciously, his hands moved to her luscious breasts and reverently stroked the tips through her modest gown. For the life of him he couldn't remember why he'd ever preferred petite, small-breasted women. Miss Somerset was like a Viking goddess, tall, strong, yet every inch a female. He could feel her quick intake of breath in response and prayed she would not pull away.

She did not.

Oh Lord, she didn't move save for the slightest trembling around her mouth. And then, very slowly, she wrapped her lovely long arms about his neck and he feared he wouldn't be able to hold on to the edges of this charade. Since when had he not been able to control the minutest of his actions in a seduction? He was dazed and slightly out of control. If she knew anything about the nature of a man's arousal, his goose was cooked.

But clearly she did not.

And then truth dawned. She was quite possibly not the fallen spinster everyone assumed. She was using none of the techniques a more seasoned lady performed naturally. She was all hesitant touches and shy maiden despite her ripe curves.

And, he was showing a lamentable lack of finesse. He was seconds away from placing her on the sand, lifting her skirts and committing the most contemptible act of his life. Worse yet, an uncomfortable, heretofore unknown sensation stirred near the cold recesses of his heart.

William had only enough wits about him to gather her up in his arms, walk knee-deep into the sea and abruptly end the lesson by dropping them

both into the icy water. He didn't once question
why he'd refrained from continuing the seduction,
the answer to all his problems.

Sophie was mortified. She sat listening to the
ranting of her maid who peeled off her drenched
and nearly ruined sandy garments. Sophie never
felt closer to tears than at that moment.

She'd humiliated herself to a degree of new
heights. Lord William had been so disgusted by her
forward behavior that he'd had to cool her ardor
by dunking her in the sea. And while her head had
been swirling with unleashed emotions, he'd voiced
worries about the effects of salt water on boots.

He'd felt nothing when they'd kissed, while she'd
been lost in a torrent of sensations. He'd only
laughed and said salt water was good for the joints
at least and then he'd abruptly halted the lesson.

Yet he'd refused to accept her plea to end the
lessons altogether. He'd said they'd both made remarkable progress, and that it was only fair she
give him his lesson at the earliest possible convenience.

Sophie shook her head. At least he'd granted her
privacy by turning his head when she'd left the
water to negotiate the climb back to Villa Belza.
And at least he'd given her enough backbone to
refuse to allow the medieval corset to ever grace
her body again. But she'd lost much in the
bargain . . . her sanity.

When she left London she'd thought her humilia-
tion absolute. Sophie closed her eyes. That wasn't
so. Complete mortification required falling in love
with a gentleman who could never ever return a
measure of her affection.

She knew why he affected her thusly. He possessed more charm than a snake, more beauty than any gentleman or lady had a right to and the most potent ingredient of all—the ability to make her laugh, something no one had accomplished in a long time.

"I must offer you some advice," Karine said, shaking her head, "for you've proved you've not a clue of how to go on."

Sophie roused herself from her reverie. Karine's advice was usually good once the barbs were removed. "Whatever do you mean?"

"You must beware of that gentleman."

"What gentleman?"

The maid made a sound of disgust. "The one you're thinking of right now. The one every female within a hundred miles dreams of. Lord William"— she cackled—"was described in France as something of a—well, something wild and exciting."

"I don't know what you are talking about, Karine."

"Baf, *alors*," she replied, shrugging her shoulders. "You can't fool me, you know. And really there's no need. You have my loyalty." Her maid smiled and resumed her task of wringing the wet garments in the basin. "Why, I've even lied for you. I told the under-footman to bring you a bath because you'd tripped and fallen into the edges of the water. The imbecile believed every word."

"What was he known as in France?"

Karine arched a brow. "*Le loup*—the wolf. And his elder brother, Viscount Gaston, was *le renard*— the fox. Some said it was because of their questionable loyalties to Napoleon, others said it was for their amorous conquests." Karine sighed and a dreamy look infused her face. "I can vouch for the appeal of the elder. I had personal experience with that divine gentleman when I was under the employ of a very stupid—uh—a Lady Susan. And my guess is Lord Will is equally devastating *in private,* if not more so." The petite maid licked her lips and looked at the ceiling, lost in apparent wicked thoughts.

"Why do you say this?"

"Ah, well, the fox, he is a social, cunning creature, is he not? The wolf, on the other hand, is a dangerous loner who runs in packs only when it suits him. And there is a certain attraction to a gentleman like that."

"Karine, I know you mean well, but, frankly I don't think you know Lord William at all. Oh, he might have taken part in the war between England and France. There are many who did. But I'm afraid Lord William isn't what you think."

A knock sounded at the door, signaling the bath water's delivery. Sophie scurried behind the screen. "And where is my cousin this morning?"

"Mr. Mornington and his sisters paid a call. The four of them decided to take the morning air in the direction of the cliffs."

Chapter Five

*I*t had been two days since William had inadvertently drunk seawater and sand while observing the delectable Miss Somerset ascend the path homeward in a wet, transparent gown that clung deliciously to her curves.

He smiled in remembrance and motioned his horse into a gallop along the road leading to the small fishing port.

She'd managed to avoid him during those two days although memories of her had not. He couldn't get the image of her out of his mind—her trusting eyes, and her laughter. And she'd provoked emotions he hadn't thought he possessed anymore.

At one point in his life he might have held a bit of romantic drivel in his heart that he had thought passed for that wilting emotion called love. He frowned at the word. But that had been for just a short while. A very short while.

A red fox dashed across the road, making his horse skitter to the side. William brought the gelding immediately back under control.

Mornington had tried to force him to desist his wooing activities when he'd confronted William two evenings ago in the masculine lair of his library.

"I'll not have it. It won't do at all. You were lucky I was able to divert my sisters and Miss Owen's attention from the beach before they spied you and Miss Somerset in that, that heated posture," Mornington had said.

"My friend, you didn't have any scruples about the lady when I first arrived. May I ask you if you are more concerned with your sisters's reactions, Miss Somerset's reputation, or is it your concern for the cousin's tender sensibilities? Is that what prompted this warning?" William had asked.

Mornington's face had turned an interesting shade of scarlet.

"*Mon Dieu,* it's as I thought. Cupid has flung his arrow and found his mark—and only after what, two or three encounters with the dark beauty? Are you ready to give up the ghost in bachelor's heaven, then?"

He had flustered Mornington almost beyond speech.

His friend had readjusted his cravat and patted his forehead with a handkerchief. "It ain't right, I tell you, for any reason. I won't try to hide anything from you. But I won't allow you to rut about in a careless fashion and ruin lives in the process."

"I'm never careless, Charles. And I promise you I won't ruin anyone's life other than my own. Perhaps I will surprise you."

Mornington had snorted his dissent.

But William had meant it.

As his horse negotiated the uneven road on this cloudless day, exhilaration coursed through his veins. Everything was falling flawlessly into place—

just like the successful days of old when he and
Farquhar had accepted assignments to ferret out
informants and thwart Napoleon's missions.

There was something stimulating in the thrill of
the chase. Walking the narrow line between success
and disaster made victory all the sweeter. His
courtship of the heiress was proving more intoxicating than he'd ever imagined.

She was in the cup of William's hand. She was
falling in love with him. He was sure. He couldn't
have mistaken the look in her eyes. And unbeliev-
ably, he was quite possibly falling in—oh, God forbid, he didn't really think that.

He doubted it would ever happen again. Besides,
that first time, in retrospect, couldn't really be
called anything but a foolish youthful passion. He
pushed his horse to gallop faster.

So what was it—that certain yearning for Sophie
Somerset, coupled with obsessive thoughts? It was
at least a surprise. And he liked surprises. William
laughed out loud, startling his horse in the process.

Who would have guessed that it would so conve-
niently fit into his pressing needs for capital? He
would be able to face Mr. Derby, and now Mr.
Thompson, and settle all the demands for funds
and approve the architectural plans for the bank.
His bank. An institution that would resurrect his
family's name once again in the highest circles of
the beau monde.

Today would be the culmination. He would declare himself, finesse any ruffled feathers over his
false appearances, and celebrate their betrothal.
And since he wasn't a slow top, he would be
damned if he didn't finagle a kiss or perhaps something more into the bargain. Not that he would

anticipate the wedding night. He was a gentleman
and far too much in command of himself to do
that, after all.

The little port of Burnham-by-the-Sea was deserted as all the men who earned their bread via
the sea's bounty had cast off in the glowing light
of dawn. Sophie readjusted her new full-length
fishing coat and again checked to make sure that
not an inch of the new pantaloons showed. She had
no desire to shock the inhabitants of the village.

But where was Mr. Seymour? The elderly parson
had promised so faithfully to go fishing with her
today. She wondered if her choice of clothes would
overly distress him. Given the amount of donations
she had made to the church, she was hopeful he
would look the other way when she removed her
coat when far from shore.

She turned at the sound of horse hooves on hardened earth.

Lord William dismounted and called a passing
boy to his aid. With the toss of a coin, the boy
took possession of the reins and led the horse away.

Oh, what was *he* doing here? And she had been
so successful in her efforts to avoid him until now.
She tried to appear unruffled by his appearance but
feared she was blushing.

"Miss Somerset, I am at your service," he said,
bowing. "It seems Mr. Seymour has pressing duties
in the parish. I offered to escort you on your fishing
expedition to relieve some of the poor man's burden. I do hope that is all right with you, ma'am?"

"Why, yes," she said, attempting to compose herself. "Yes, of course, my lord." Was there no excuse she could invent on short notice? How was a
day spent alone with him to be borne? "But, really,

I would not inconvenience you. I think I shall wait for another day. And I now remember that Mr. Mornington and Mari mentioned their interest in fishing as well."

"Mornington, spend the day fishing? I don't believe the man has ever set foot in a boat again after becoming violently seasick on his grand tour."

"Oh, I see."

"Now then, do you have everything we will need? Tackle, bait, refreshments?" His eyes held a glint of amusement.

She thought frantically. Before she could reply, he had taken his decision.

"Good. Then we're off." He leaned down to reposition the small boat on the ramp. The next moment, he launched the fishing vessel from the moss-covered slope into the sea. Sophie hopped into it at the last moment, and he followed her, taking up the oars to put some distance from the shore.

"I thought this might be the perfect opportunity, *chérie*," he said, "for your promised lessons on, let's see—Character, Distaste for dandies, and wasn't it also, the Error of my ways?"

She found he was looking directly at her when she dared to raise her eyes. His eyes crinkled in the corners.

"Why yes, that would be an excellent topic for today, my lord."

"Do you think you could find it in your heart to call me 'William'? 'My lord' sounds so, so formal. We've become great friends, haven't we?"

"Perhaps, but I think I'd better not. I shall try to avoid any use of your name at all, in future, as I don't want to offend."

He was rowing with expert dexterity. Evidently,

he had spent a good deal of time around boats. It was in conflict with his usual dandyish existence. But now that she had somewhat regained her wits she noticed he was dressed in much more somber, practical clothing than usual.

It was unmercifully hot. He stopped rowing for a moment to peel off his bottle green coat.

She felt awkward, watching him work the oars. The great muscles in his tall frame strained against his shirt. And the muscles in his long legs . . . well, they were straining too. Sophie forced herself to look at the water. She dragged her hand alongside the boat to cool herself. She didn't dare take off her coat.

"*Chérie,* the sun is blazing. Really, you should remove that heavy coat," he said.

"I'm perfectly comfortable, my lord."

"You're afraid to show me your pantaloons, then. There's no need to be embarrassed. I'm well familiar with your female form already and you've nothing to fear from me. Truly, I've your best interests at heart." He sported a poorly disguised sly grin.

Wretched man. "Why am I not surprised by your lamentable lack of talent in putting a lady at ease?"

He laughed.

The heat and humidity was causing William's lawn shirt to stick to the contours of his broadly muscled chest. All at once she was dizzy. Perhaps it was the heat, more likely it was the sudden remembrance of his chiseled, steaming form, naked from the bath.

In disgust, she took off her coat.

"Ah, *chérie,* that's much better. And it also serves to increase my desire—"

She inhaled sharply.

"—to finish the job of rowing to the cove." He winked at her. "If I really wanted to embarrass you, I'd tell you that you look like the goddess Diana the Huntress in those delightfully snug pantaloons."

Sophie couldn't think of a single way to lead him off the topic and sincerely hoped silence would do the trick.

He'd put a good deal of distance between them and the shore and finally they were within a few oar strokes of the cove.

"Do you know if the fishing is good here?" she asked.

"I have the port master's word on it," he replied. "It also has the added benefit of being secluded. And I'm in need of a private audience with you."

What?

"I beg your pardon?" What was he about? Oh, why couldn't he be serious and refrain from ridiculous innuendo?

"Patience, *chérie,* patience."

He stopped rowing suddenly. They drifted among the small swells, wavelets lapping against the sides of the little boat.

She reached for one of the fishing rods.

"No, you must hear me out now, my darling, for I've something of importance to tell you. Then you shall have your day of fishing, if you desire it still." His lips curved into the familiar devastating smile.

Sophie shivered. *My darling?*

And then Lord Will leaned forward to grasp her hands in his own. They were warm and very solid.

"Sophie, darling," he murmured. "Surely, you have guessed that I've become . . . fond of you?"

At the use of her given name, a flutter of excitement shook her. He was playing a game, trying to make her laugh.

"You are deliciously refreshing," he continued. "Truly a lady different in almost every respect from other females I've known. Your goodness, indeed, your character, and your courage and honesty intrigue me."

Sophie finally dared look him full in the face again. His deep voice, and heavy-lidded eyes resonated her senses.

"In fact"—he arched an eyebrow—"I do believe, I'm fall— No, I cannot say such romantic nonsense in daylight. And I doubt an impassioned, overused sentiment will make you swoon into my arms." He lowered his voice. "You shall just have to wait to hear it under the covers." His dimples appeared alongside his dazzling white smile and he winked.

What?

Lord William tilted his head and waited. "I do believe this is the part where you're supposed to throw your arms about me and declare your undying love in return, *chérie*," he said. "But I suppose it's too much to ask in this unsteady vessel."

Surely, she imagined what he'd just said. His lips had moved, but he couldn't have implied he was in love with her. Her body grew cold despite the sun.

"Perhaps," he continued, "you're convinced my character is so beyond salvation that I'm proposing marriage in an attempt to win our little wager? *Chérie,* I would be more than willing to wear fisherman's rags in Hyde Park for at the least, let's say, a week—although I hope you would take pity before that—if you do me the honor of becoming my wife."

Sophie recovered sufficiently to speak. "Your wife?" she asked faintly.

He leaned forward and patted her hand before cupping her face with his warm fingers. "My darling, I hadn't thought it would be such a shock. Had you not guessed of my change of heart?"

"But what of Mr. Farquhar?" she asked.

"Why, he'll be delighted when I tell him."

"But I thought you and he were . . ." *No she would not, could not, say it.*

"Were what, *chérie*?"

She stared at him.

"Did you assume we had more than just a servant-master connection? Hmmmm, and I was just remarking on your excellent character. I've known Jack Farquhar for over a decade and a half, my darling. We met at a most provident time, when we were both independently captured during a mission. I discovered Farquhar's excellent acting abilities and devious mind—both very useful when we decided to join forces working in secret for the Crown."

Sophie plucked at her pantaloons. "But, then, you tricked me. You allowed me to believe you were attracted to . . ."

"Say no more, my darling. You've cured me of every failing and I will promise to avoid falsehoods in future and remain faithful to you, always." His posture oozed charm and confidence.

"And you probably lied to me about the parson. Did you pay him to get me alone again?"

"Now, Sophie, I thought this would be a most roman—"

"Why you're the most pompous, self-important, presumptuous . . . *ass*! You expect me to accept a marriage proposal from you after you've deceived me, tricked me and even entered into a false wager with me? You know nothing about me, sir. I wouldn't have you if you were the last man on earth!"

"My, my, *chérie,* your language. You don't want to show your origins, dearest," he said, sure of his eventual success. "Now let's be serious, for I think if we joined—"

With that, Sophie took an oar, stood up and pushed at his chest with the paddle. The angle and force were enough to make him lose his balance on the high, narrow bench. His eyes widened in surprise as he toppled head over heels into the sea. The only reminder of male arrogance was his tall beaver hat floating on the bubbling water.

Sophie took enormous satisfaction watching him bobble to the surface, and gasp for air. "And in case you didn't fully comprehend my signal, Lord Will, in the language of the *oar*—not the fan, mind you—that means, 'Stay away from me, you, you puffed-up imposter, if you treasure your life.'"

He treaded water while simultaneously attempting to remove his heavy boots. "Have a heart, Sophie," he said laughing. "Take pity on a drowning man! On the man who adores you and will father your children."

"Not on my life," she said. "I don't have pity for lying devils."

"Well, at least I've risen a notch in your estimation over the last minute. A devil is at least a human form . . ." He stopped when he saw the fury in her face. "I shall make it my mission in life to earn your good opinion, darling."

She grabbed the two oars and began rowing back to the shore in earnest.

Well, he thought, as he began swimming to the beach, the idea of a post-engagement celebratory kiss had been, perhaps, a bit optimistic. It seemed that, indeed, hell hath no fury like a woman . . . deceived.

No matter. She loved him and he would have her in the end. Her initial refusal just heightened his interest. Ah, she was a true delight and they would share a wonderful life together once he wooed her back. And he hadn't a doubt he would accomplish it.

Had he not spent the better part of his adulthood charming females of all types into his arms? And success would be all the sweeter with this briefest of missteps.

The score stood, one for his sweet Sophie and one for the devil.

Chapter Six

*T*he dinner party at Villa Belza was as uncomfortable as Sophie had imagined it would be. During the entire five courses and removes, Lord Will refrained from saying a single word to her.

He barely even looked at her.

Well, at least he had taken her refusal seriously.

And he took obvious comfort in the bevy of females at the far end of the table who besieged him.

The day after their encounter in the boat, Sophie had deemed it wise to add another family to the long-promised gathering the next evening. There was safety to be had in numbers lest she be forced to converse with the snake and do him harm. And so she'd sent a late invitation to the Aversleys of Bath, to whom Aunt Rutledge had insisted Sophie pay a courtesy call while in the country. This would relieve her social obligation.

Unfortunately, the evening hadn't transpired as planned, like all of the events of her life as of late.

The Aversley party consisted of only six persons. Aside from the fiftyish or so father, of the leering eyes, there was the tiny, meek-minded mother, their three daughters and one son of fifteen given to coughing fits. The three older sons of the Aversleys had been forced to remain at home due to the same illness that obviously affected the younger son. So much for balancing the numbers.

The daughters were quite beautiful and the Mornington sisters took an instant envy and dislike to them. The same could not be said for Lord William.

Sophie had never seen so many females fighting mind and body over one male. And the Aversley ladies, much to the dismay of the Mornington girls, had the upper hand with their superior beauty and intelligence.

"Lord Will, do tell us about your daring deeds during the war. My father was well acquainted with several officers at the top levels of British intelligence. Papa said you were one of the fiercest spies in France," Miss Aversley said, fluttering her eyelashes down over her wide, round eyes the color of bluebells. The lady's bright auburn curls fell in soft waves about her heart-shaped face. She was one of the prettiest females Sophie had ever seen. Her sisters were even more perfect if it was possible.

He raised his hands as if to speak, displayed his most seductive smile and shook his head.

"Oh, Lord William, you can count on us to be the souls of discretion. We would not breathe a word to anyone," sighed Miss Anna Mornington.

"Oh, yes, do tell us more of your life, my lord," said Miss Philippa Aversley, the only brunette in the family. "Your exploits and heroic efforts are well known to us."

Sophie could almost hear a collective sigh of rapture from every female breast in the room save hers and Mari's.

She was beginning to feel rather ill at the sight of all these females hanging on to the scraps of stories and attention Lord William tossed their way.

Sophie was stuck between the coughing boy and his lecherous father. Really! What had her aunt been thinking? And Mari and Mr. Mornington were so wrapped up in each other's conversation they provided no diversion whatsoever.

But God finally took pity on her at the end of the meal when the boy exhibited a particularly long paroxysm and it was decided the family must return to Bath despite the near-to-tears expressions of the pretty sisters.

The remaining members of the party, with the exception of Lord Will, breathed a sigh of relief when the Aversleys departed. The residents of Burnham-by-the-Sea then retired to the elegant music room.

"Miss Somerset, you've been remarkably generous in your attentions to the neighborhood, from the donations for the restoration of the school to all your visits to the infirm," Mr. Mornington said.

Sophie, in front of the tea and coffee service in the large room, refilled his proffered cup.

Mr. Mornington continued, "You're more than filling the role of the former Duchess of Cornwallis. I cannot tell you how sad my family, indeed the entire county, was when news of the duke and duchess's deaths in London reached us so soon after their son's death. My mother counted the duchess as her closest friend. We spent so many happy hours here, visiting the villa."

"I know little of my uncle and aunt's ties." She swallowed awkwardly.

"My mother and Her Grace attended school together and remained like sisters to one another their entire lives, writing to each other most faithfully when they were apart. I am sorry you didn't know your uncle and aunt."

"I am too, sir."

"Her Grace would have been so happy to know of your good works in the neighborhood."

"Please don't go on, Mr. Mornington," she replied. "My father always said acts of charity should remain anonymous or else they'll not count when one rattles the pearly gates."

She looked up to find Lord Will grinning at her. He was again dressed in somber attire. Gone were the ruffles, lace and flamboyant colors. Elegant buff breeches, a dark blue superfine coat and top boots had taken their place. Unfortunately, his staggering handsomeness remained to torment her.

"Do you have anything to fear, my dear, when you face St. Peter?" he asked.

"I'm sure I've far less to fear than you, my lord."

He smiled again, revealing those roguish dimples of his. "A hit, mademoiselle. You know not how you wound me." His dark eyes twinkled and Sophie's stomach turned over.

There was a reason she'd refused to see him when he'd called and left his card the day before. She could name about a thousand reasons, starting with those eyes of his and ending with his devious nature.

Sophie turned to glance at Mari, seated in the alcove of the music room. The glass doors were open, refreshing the room that had remained closed off for many months. The sounds of early summer crickets filled the chamber as well as a slight breeze, which teased the corners of the striped silk curtains.

Mr. Mornington rejoined her cousin to enjoy a quiet tête-à-tête. The Misses Mornington were too far away to come to her aid. They were locked in a heated battle over who would play the pianoforte first.

"I'm afraid you're stuck with me, *chérie,* for conversation. But that's no great hardship, is it? We've always been able to amuse one another," Lord Will said in low tones.

Sophie inhaled. But before she could answer him, he continued. "Have you been thinking about our last encounter? Ah, I see by your expression that you have."

She forced her hands to remain calmly folded in her lap. "Only insofar as I didn't have the opportunity to tell you more precisely what I really think of you. But at least I won't feel the need to teach you the proposed lessons—about Character, or perhaps Conscience, and the rest. For I think we both know that would be a completely wasted effort."

"I am sorry to hear that. I'd not thought you would try to end our wager unfairly. You take much pride in your good character and reneging on a bet does not sit well. And I offered the perfect solution."

Surely, she would explode in anger.

Mari returned to refill her teacup. Sophie threw in two lumps of sugar with enough fury that the tea splashed over the rim of the delicate porcelain.

"I am so sorry, Mari. Do let me give you another cup."

"Don't go to the trouble, dearest," Mari said, barely noticing. And then she focused on Sophie's discomfort. "Are you all right, cousin? You're flushed."

Sophie gritted out an assurance of good health and Mari wandered back to her prince.

"*Chérie,* I would not see you so upset. Your happiness is my primary concern."

"If that is so, then you'll take yourself out of my sight before I say something I shall regret." She smiled at Mr. Mornington who was watching her.

"That's an excellent idea. What we need is seclusion, *chérie,* to resolve all the issues that stand in the way of our happy future."

"Well, I think you'd be better served if you looked for your happy future in Bath where three Aversley females will hang on your every word and shower you with adoration for the rest of your life."

He chuckled. "I knew you loved me," he whispered and fingered a tendril of hair that had come loose from the coiffure Karine had arranged hours ago.

"What!"

"Very good. I shall return later this evening, when we can be alone and I can revel in those seeds of jealousy by planting my—"

"That is out of the question."

"*Chérie,* you're adorable when you're in a pique. Promise you will argue with me at least once a week when we are wed."

She was silent, looking beyond his shoulder.

"No? I see you fear I'm not taking you seriously. When I return I promise I'll listen to every loathsome word you hurl my way and then we'll have our heart-to-heart." He paused. "There is something of vital importance I must give you."

"I will not accept anything from you."

"I promise you'll not break any rule accepting this token. Quite the contrary, *chérie.*"

He discreetly picked up her hand and a curl of heat flowed to her breast.

"I also promise I'll not place you in any type of danger for even the slightest moment. My word."

"The path to hell is paved with broken promises."

"I thought it was paved with good intentions."

"In your case they're one and the same, sir."

"Ah, you are . . . perhaps correct," he said, surprising her with his answer.

Mari walked up with Mr. Mornington in time to save Sophie from trying to outwit Lord William. "Has my cousin said something to offend, my lord?"

Mr. Mornington appeared mesmerized by Mari whose hand gently rested on top of the stout gentleman's arm. All at once her partner spoke. "That's all right, Miss Somerset, Lord Will often provokes extreme retaliation. I'm sure you're not to blame."

"Mr. Mornington"—Sophie smiled up to his pleasing countenance—"Lord William is our guest, and as such, should be accorded every *courtesy* due him. In fact, I should make a greater effort to be a better hostess to all of you."

It was so easy after that. She flittered about and engaged in conversation with everyone. Turning the pages of music for both the Misses Mornington proved to be the best possible employment. The Mornington sisters murdered the music quite exquisitely. There were copious missed notes and Sophie was gratified that the music was altogether too loud to permit much discussion.

"Did you know Lord Will composes music, Miss Somerset?" Miss Mornington pulled a small sheath of musical score from her voluminous reticule. "I brought this copy of a sonata he gave to my mother many years ago when he came to Hinton Arms on holiday one summer. I've been practicing it to play for him. I shall surprise him," she continued, excitement filling her face.

"I don't remember Lord Will ever playing music for us," Felicia Mornington said, annoyed. "I would've remembered."

"Not at all, Licia. You were still a mere infant, three or four years old to my seven years. And I remember it well. Charles and Lord Will both turned fifteen on Midsummer's Eve and were allowed to dine with the adults, leaving us to dine alone." She pouted in remembrance, then continued. "And Lord Will wrote this for Mama because she loved to hear him play." Anna Mornington clearly enjoyed lording over her seniority at every opportunity. "And father forbade Mama to play the sonata after the boys returned to Eton. But it is so beautiful, I will play it for everyone."

The girl began keying the haunting score. Sadly, she made many jarring mistakes and rushed the piece.

The younger sister jumped to her feet and went to Lord William. "Really, we should ask you to perform. My sister tells me you play like no one else." She giggled, and fluttered her eyelashes before him.

He turned to Sophie. "I—I am certain we've exhibited enough talent for one evening." He wore a curious remote expression, which was replaced within moments by his usual charming yet superior air. "I think it best we take our leave. I believe we have long outstayed our welcome. And—the sooner we go, the sooner we will have the pleasure of seeing you in future." He clasped her hand and raised it to his lips.

Mari was flustered by the mention of a departure. "Oh, but it is much too early for leave-taking, surely. We have not even set out the card tables yet." She had no eyes for anyone save Mr. Mornington.

That gentleman glanced at his pocket watch, then at Sophie almost sheepishly. "His lordship's correct. We've forgotten we're outside of London and, as such, should adhere to country hours."

Another disappointment was voiced from behind the pianoforte. Only the strongest stare from the brother silenced the sister. With the briefest of words, and the longest of glances between Mari and her smitten swain, the party from Hinton Arms took their leave.

Mari begged fatigue with a glow of happiness on her face, but Sophie wasn't in a good enough humor to follow her upstairs to hear for the umpteenth time Mr. Mornington's praises. Instead, she returned to the music room.

She could have no more stayed away from the sheets of music still propped above the pianoforte's keys than a moth resists a flame. It had been months since she had played, a lifetime ago it seemed. She hadn't had the heart to try this magnificent instrument because it would bring back poignant memories of playing the pianoforte at home for her father who had loved to hear her play.

She stared at the bold strokes of notes on the page, hearing the music in her mind.

Softly, ever so softly, she stroked the keys. The lilting music began so achingly sweet and simple. It then rose higher and higher in such passionate intensity that it was almost impossible to play.

Sophie was amazed Lord Will had composed it. Could it be possible that there was perhaps just the smallest bit more to Lord William than met the eye? And yet he had refused to play, which went against his usual preening character. Was there something beyond the façade he presented? Perhaps a shocking flicker of humility deep beneath the veneer?

Sophie shut her eyes and stilled her hands on the keys. She was obsessed with thoughts of him again. It was ridiculous. She was reading into his minutest actions implausible ideas. He had had that strange expression after the piece was played because the Mornington sisters had played so long, and so ill that it had given him the same headache she now had herself.

He was returning to his chambers probably to dissect the sheer stupidity of the evening to his, his devoted man, Mr. Farquhar. And they would laugh as they drank brandy and waved about their fans with only Mrs. Tickle to bear witness to their merriment.

He had said he would come—tonight—for some sort of clandestine rendezvous. More likely he was laughing, picturing her waiting up for him in the shadows of the front hall. He was undoubtedly telling his valet how she wore her heart on her sleeve and how he was tiring of acting the eager lover.

Sophie was sure Lord Will was perceptive enough about the human condition to know that her professed hatred was as obsessive as love and frequently could be reversed most thoroughly.

She had failed miserably at acting the lassitude of a truly disinterested party. And so he would continue to pursue her and wear her down and she wasn't sure she would be able to resist him.

There was just the smallest part of her ego that was screaming in her head that maybe, just maybe he *had* fallen in love with her. Opposites did attract. Her father had told her that many times. She was sure, on several occasions, such as the one tonight, she had glimpsed something more in his eyes than just amusement. It hinted at strong emotions and sometimes, of something darker, more vulnerable.

Or perhaps it was just pure deviltry. She would not put it past him to have wagered that he would have her, and to make a game of it. It was much more likely.

But one did not deceive the person one loved. She would never fully understand the devious machinations of the members of the beau monde. But why the trickery?

He was so handsome, titled and supremely eligible. He could have his choice of almost any lady.

Sophie shivered.

She was going to have to go away again. She was going to have to write a letter to Aunt Rutledge and tell her that she was returning to Porthcall. She had put it off long enough. She was never going to be able to return to London. And, really, she didn't care about that silly wager she had made with his lordship. She would leave without a word, to avoid listening to his boasts at having her forfeit the bet.

It was not that he didn't like her, but simply that his amused affection for her would torment her if she stayed since her sensibilities ran so much deeper. He obviously had nothing better to do, lolling about the countryside and taking pleasure in ridiculous games to fill his time frivolously. Well, she would not go along.

The hair on the back of her head prickled. She sensed someone's presence. Sophie swung around from the bench and saw no one. All at once, she spied a man's shadow at the open glass doors leading to the terrace.

Sophie held her breath and rose from her seat.

She stared at the dark profile. A hand rose to the face and the bright orange tip of a cheroot glowed.

It was he.

"You are a liar, *chérie*," he said, quietly. He stirred from his hiding place in the shadows of the doorway. "You play well."

"What are you doing here? This is highly improper."

"I was hoping you would be more original," he said dryly.

Lord Will slowly strode into full view at the doorframe, throwing the cheroot into the pea gravel walk behind.

"I'm sorry to disappoint, but you must leave. I can't be found alone with you."

He walked through the music room to the door leading to the hallway and turned the key.

Sophie shivered and stroked her arms when she heard the loud click of the lock engaging.

"So much for your fears, *chérie*." Lord Will came toward her, his heels clicking on the parquet floor. He moved next to her on the bench, casually flicking his coat tails behind him as he sat next to her and posed his hands above the keys.

"You almost had it right. Only the last part was ill played," he said.

Sophie scooted to the other end of the bench, her skin scorched by the contact of his large thigh and arm brushing hers. She watched his beautiful hands poised over the instrument and her heart constricted.

He began to play the music with a level of expertise Sophie had rarely, if ever, witnessed. Perhaps there might have been some soloist at a musicale in London who rivaled his talent, but she doubted it.

He was a master.

He built from the light, joyful beginning to a crescendo of intense magnitude. The music then became mournful and haunting in the finale. It spoke of longing and seemed to end with a question. His hands dropped from the keys.

She stared at him. This was the dishonest dandified fop of a man who cared only for frivolity and games? There had to be something more, only a man of strong, real emotions and vast intelligence could have composed and played music such as this. Oh yes, there was a good deal more.

He sat, his eyes closed, his head dropped forward, in deep thought. He opened his eyes and looked at her. For just the slightest moment she beheld an expression of such profound intensity that the revealed emotion and veiled vulnerability was almost painful to witness. And then it was gone, replaced by his usual expression. He reassumed the aristocratic tilt to his head, half closed his eyes and smiled.

"*Alors,* I've pleased you with this serenade, *chérie*?"

He leaned toward her and brushed a gentle kiss on her cheek, then moved closer. "Have I won your respect? Perhaps it is enough to have earned your much promised lesson?" he asked.

"Why are you here, my lord?" Sophie whispered. She turned her attention to the piano keys and gently rubbed one.

He paused in his reply. "Why, I told you I would return—bearing gifts no less."

He inched closer again, the heat of him tantalizing her senses. She felt suspended in time as she watched him pull an object from his breast pocket. It glittered in the candlelight.

"Sophie, I daresay I went about it all wrong yesterday. And so, I'm asking you to reconsider, my darling. I apologize for deceiving you. And yes, I freely admit I was a complete oaf in all my actions. But I must also declare that I am falling, rather amazingly I must add, *in love with you* and I desire to make you my wife. I'm determined to make you mine."

Sophie could not say a word. She looked at the beautiful sapphire and diamond ring he held before her in his long, elegant fingers.

"This was my mother's ring, given to her by my father on the occasion of their betrothal. Will you accept it? I promise to make your happiness my mission in life," he continued. "Let us give all the gossipmongers of London the juiciest tidbit of their lives to chew over. They'll say the daughter of a Welsh vicar has finally tamed the notorious rogue using her natural goodness and honesty to enslave him. Undoubtedly, we'll be doing a good turn for all the other bachelors in town as chits will then attempt to employ your novel methods."

He paused to sweep behind her ear a lock of hair that had fallen. "Darling, I find myself rambling along here, hoping you will look at me at some point so I can see in your eyes if you plan to make me the happiest of men tonight."

She squeezed her eyes shut and took a deep breath. She finally looked at him.

"Oh, my love. No, don't . . ." he said gently. "There's no need for tears. If you intend to reject me, I would much rather face your wrath. I am no good at tears."

She tried to hold back, but felt one tear escape down the hot flesh of her face.

"Sophie, for God's sake, say something. Do you want me to leave? I shall if you insist. Darling . . . I'm so sorry I hurt you. I've never been much good at exposing my heart and the rest as I suppose I didn't see much goodness until you, my sweet Sophie. I promise I shall never hurt you ever again. And I pledge a most glorious life together." He finally pulled her into his arms and forced her head to rest on his wide chest.

He smelled of night air, and tobacco, and that wonderful masculine scent that was him. She couldn't resist. It, he, everything was surreal and intoxicating.

She loved him.

And he loved her.

She was sure.

She would not let pride stand in her way. She had never really had much pride anyway. There had been little use for it in her life in Porthcall. Only the rich could afford pride.

She pulled away from him and opened her clenched hands. Blood rushed back into the aching palms where her nails had bitten into her flesh.

"I accept your offer," she said softly, offering her hand. "I should be happy to marry you and I shall promise to forget our unfortunate beginning."

"My darling, I will make every effort to measure up to your standards of the best of husbands."

Her heart surged with indefinable joy. She could not fully accept it. He loved her after all. Oh, perhaps it had started out as a game to him, but it had ended differently than he had most likely envisioned.

She was her father's daughter, and forgiveness was her forte. She would forget his silly trickery, and remember only the laughter, and growing tenderness they had shared.

She looked at his expression and saw devotion.

And then he was embracing her. He kissed her cheeks, then her nose, her eyelids and finally the sensitive corner of her lips. Sophie tried to regulate her breathing, and failed.

He brushed his mouth against hers once, twice, three times and then enveloped her lips with his own. She was aware of the heated inner flesh of his mouth and opened herself to him.

His tongue brushed against hers and she felt as if she was falling, falling. The taste of brandy, and cheroots and of him entered into the maelstrom playing havoc with her senses. Sophie could barely control the feeling coursing through her as he left a trail of kisses from her mouth to her neck, to the edges of her gown.

She breathed deeply as he nudged the lace fichu at her neckline aside and ran his hand over the curve of her breast.

For a moment, sanity almost returned and she thought about the necessity of putting an end to this. It occurred when he readjusted their seating. But it was only the briefest instant. He swept her onto his lap in one powerful motion. And then she was lost again in a sea of the most potent longing she had ever known.

Sophie tried to stop the trembling of her body but could not. She was unable to resist the sensations he released each time he was alone with her.

"Stop me," he whispered. "For God's sake, Sophie, stop me."

She shivered. There was such intensity in his command. But his poignant expression begged for just the opposite.

She shook her head slowly.

She would give of herself to him because of the intense need she read in his gaze. And so she overcame her shyness and did not resist her innate desire to soothe those who suffered. She had never seen such a raw ache as she glimpsed deep in the loneliness of his soul.

What had happened to him? What had put that pain and piercing cynicism in his true spirit, the one beyond the jaded aristocratic façade? Sophie responded to his anguish the only way she knew, by offering comfort and love.

Again, he passed his hand over the low bodice of her gown, this time easing the corner buttons from the hollows of her shoulders. The front flap of the gown opened and he brushed away the chemise. Sophie watched as he took the rosy tip of her breast between his full lips.

Oh, his mouth was so warm, and wet, and he was making a pulling sensation and doing something with his tongue and teeth that made her want to faint.

His dark hair slipped through her fingers as her head dropped back in mute acquiescence. He kissed and caressed her breasts in ways too sinful to contemplate. All the while, the coarseness of his whiskers teased her sensitive skin.

Sitting in his lap, she slowly became conscious of a thickness jutting from him. With deep embarrassment, she sensed dampness and an ache between her limbs. What was happening to her?

When she dared to reopen her eyes, it had become so dark in the room. All but one candle had guttered on the wall sconce beside her.

He abruptly lifted his lips and gently blew on the tip of her breast, sending tingling sensations throughout her body. His hands caressed her as gently as newly unfurled butterfly's wings.

He raised his eyes to hers and looked at her for a long moment, appearing starkly coherent, and deadly serious. A searing tension filled the air between them, pulling her inexorably closer to him.

She could not look away. She stared back at him, drinking in the sight of his impossibly handsome and mysterious face.

He looked as if he was about to say something, but at the last minute, he said nothing at all. Instead he continued to stare at her while he began a more intimate exploration of her body.

Sophie felt the large warm imprint of one of his large calloused hands on her ankle. He was gathering the fabric of her gown in bunches to her lap. His hand touched the underside of her knee, then her thigh, raising gooseflesh along the way.

She felt her grip on the reality of the moment loosen as he lightly, oh so lightly, caressed the top of her thigh and lowered his lips to her own, finally, once again.

Sophie was lost.

Chapter Seven

*W*illiam was lost.

Perhaps he could have stopped himself if he had not looked at her wide gray-green eyes every few moments. He felt drunk, looking at the depths of feelings he found reflected there.

He knew without a doubt they were sharing a moment out of time. A moment they would never forget the rest of their lives—when they had both let down the last of their defenses to find an equally shared joy in their passion for one another. This was not an encounter sexual in nature. It was entirely more intimate and unnerving.

He had come home. She was his home, now and forever more. The one he had lost as a young boy—for home was not a place, but a feeling.

He pushed aside the thin white shift fabric with his palm to caress her inner thigh one last time. Then he gently, tenderly slid his hand forward to the place that was sure to drive them both to madness.

She made the smallest sound in her throat and trembled.

"Sophie, you must stop me now. I cannot do this to you. I don't want to hurt you, my love."

"No, my—my dearest William. It is I who do this

to you." She whispered it so quietly he had to dip his head to catch her words.

The sound of his name broke him. He gathered her tightly to his chest and stood up. His glance swept the room, searching for a place for them. In five long strides he found himself before a long, brown velvet chaise lounge where upon he placed his Sophie.

She was so beautiful, the creamy expanse of her breasts, her long, slender legs, the dreamy, loving expression on her face. She reached her hand out to him, looking every inch like Venus reincarnate.

There was a certain desperate nature to his wanting her. Gone from his mind were all the subtle seduction techniques he had used with much success over the years. A primal need to possess her surged through his body, refusing to allow his mind to function in its steady, methodical manner.

He fumbled with his buttoned flap, a curse under his breath. He lay between her long, slender thighs and rested his forehead against her shoulder, gulping a great lungful of air.

His hand sought the entrance to her and he stroked her, gliding along the folds and finally pressing his palm firmly against her. He gently entered her with one long finger and felt her inner muscles clench against him. Moving rhythmically, and slowly inside of her, he listened to her sighs.

And suddenly a sort of cold calm invaded his body. He kissed her, and raised his head to look down at her. "My Sophie, I am about to take possession of you, you know that, don't you?"

"That is what we have both been doing to each other all along, isn't it?" Her voice, so innocent and yet womanly did not waver for a moment. "Come to me, my love. Let me hold you."

She touched him then, urging him to take her. Her fingers, timid and unsure, were more erotic than any skilled courtesan's and his manhood had never felt so swollen with need. He squeezed his eyes shut and didn't move. His size often over-whelmed women and he had never dared to lie with a virgin. He hated the idea of hurting her.

William felt a warm, constant pressure on his back and the backs of his legs and finally under-stood that it was Sophie's long arms and legs urging him to mount her.

He raised himself to meet her and instinctively placed just the tip of himself inside her. He felt heat and wetness, and his groin tightened to a pres-sure unknown in its intensity.

Yet he could not make himself move.

Again, he felt the pressure of Sophie's arms and legs, and heard soft cooing in his ear.

He pushed just the slightest fraction of an inch more inside of her and realized he was having great difficulty breathing. His heart raced and he couldn't speak to her, comfort her, tell her all the sentiments he should.

She was not only his love, she was everything he had forgotten about in his thirty-five years.

Her soft sounds of encouragement stopped and her breaths came in short gasps. He had placed too much weight on her. Oh, everything was going all wrong. He was hurting her. She was so moist and warm, yet his size was much too large for her un-tried passage. He forced himself to speak. "Sophie, my love, I'm so sorry."

Her response was to pull him tighter toward her, deeper within her. There was an awful sensation of slow tearing while his length forged its way past her maidenhead to the very core of her.

He suddenly felt very much like crying for the only time in his life.

"I am yours, William. Now and forever," she whispered into his ear.

His seed burst from him in an endless, long series of spasms. It felt like a transferal of part of the essence of his spirit.

It had not been remotely like any encounter he had ever had with a female. For a few fleeting seconds he had removed the iron curtain he used to cover his true self. And he revolted against the idea of revealing any part of himself to anyone. That involved trust, a certain vulnerable weakness he had discarded early in life. No, this had not been pleasant.

The times he had had carnal relations with women in the past had been slow, sensual, pleasurable, mutually satisfying, invigorating. He had explored and exceeded every delight that could be performed on the body. He had mindlessly pleasured his bed partners and they had eagerly pleasured him in return, filling him with an ill-gotten sort of satisfaction. Fornication, in short.

But, this had been a release. It had liberated him from his past connections and it bound him to a future unlike anything he had imagined.

Yet, he had hurt her. He had not taken her innocence in the proper, least painful way. He should have touched her, tasted her, massaged her for many, many long minutes. Instead it had been she who had comforted him. He felt indebted to her— an uncomfortable, weak sensibility.

When the long pulses of his body stopped, he gathered her in his arms and rested against her. She smelled faintly of roses.

She was gliding her palms up and down the

length of the back of his coat. Good God, he hadn't even removed an article of his clothing. She quietly said his name, and a stream of soothing words spoke of loving devotion.

It was so tight and inviting inside of her, he could not stop his arousal from hardening again into a need more familiar than before. He grasped her hand and moved it to his lips, kissing it and noticing the deep fire of the sapphire now resting on her finger.

His took his first full, long stroke within her and felt her quick intake of breath. This would be all for her.

His mind had returned and he used every last skill he knew to bring her to the brink of pleasure. He touched her with his deft fingers, and his mouth, always stroking into her slowly, expertly, for a very long time until he knew, without doubt, that she would find her release.

He pushed himself as deeply as he dared, filling her completely and yet encouraging her body to take even more of himself inside her. And when he felt the pulsing of her muscles, he held himself rigidly still, then stretched her even more to bring her fulfillment for as long as possible.

When she was quiet, he raised himself on his arms and looked down at her. She was dazed and exhausted, on the brink of sleep. He kissed her forehead and gathered her back into his arms, making sure to take as much weight off of her as he could.

She sighed and was asleep in moments.

His arousal was now painful and still deep and full within her. He regulated his breathing and slowly, ever so slowly withdrew from her. He did not even try to understand why he refused himself this second release.

He understood so little of what had overcome him. There was only one thing he understood with crystal clarity. He had been entirely wrong to think that he was master and commander of this match.

Sophie tiptoed up the servant's stair in the darkness to avoid the dozing footmen at the main staircase. Shoes in one hand, touching the thin banister railing with the other, she silently crept to her bedchamber. Each step proved an effort as she was swollen and sore where William had been.

Sophie prayed her smug maid had refused to wait up as she would be unable to bear Karine's knowing eyes.

The chamber's latch screeched long and loud when she moved the intricate brass lever. Sophie peeked around the edge of the door to find Karine seated before Sophie's little gilt table, littered with articles from Sophie's personal toilette. Her maid was trying the new subtle rouge she had forced Sophie to buy in London. The one Sophie had disdained to wear. Karine's appraising glance reflected from the oval looking glass.

"It is as I thought," the pretty, petite maid stated matter-of-factly. "Let us remove that gown before any stains set."

Sophie knew she was blushing, but refused to speak as Karine rose from her perch to remove the gown.

"I tried to warn you, mademoiselle, did I not?" Karine gathered Sophie's dress in her arms and moved to hang it near the basin, her hips swaying with every step. "But do they listen? Never. They all think, 'I am a lady and a gentleman would never dare to compromise me.' Well, it happens everyday. Just tell me you didn't believe him when he told you he was falling in love with you, did you?"

Sophie blinked.

"Ah, I see that you did. You then, take the prize of being the most naive of the lot I have served."

Her maid then uttered a long string of French words that Sophie could only guess were ineptitudes being heaped on her gullible head.

"And did he play the piano for you, too? I have heard that he plays remarkably well. He has a special sonata he uses when he attempts the seduction. Ah, he used that on you also? Well—at least you had the chance to experience the ultimate seduction from the ultimate rogue. There are many who would envy you. But they all hold one important distinction. They are all *married or widowed* and therefore not so silly as you. It is said below stairs at Hinton Arms that he generally prefers petite beauties with youthful physiques, much like me," Karine added, looking down to admire her own tiny frame.

Sophie's heart plummeted. "Stop, Karine. Stop this instant. I cannot stand another word."

"But I'm only trying to tell you what you'll need to—"

"I don't need to win him over. He has proposed marriage. We're to be wedded as soon as the banns are read. We have only left to decide if it will be done here or at St. George's. My aunt told me a long time ago that she had her heart set on a huge town wedding for me."

Karine had always been adept at demoralizing her. This had been the most magnificent night of her life and instead she now felt deflated. She tried hard not to listen to Karine. She didn't want the black tentacles of doubt to unfurl in her consciousness. Had her acceptance of his proposal and their passionate encounter been nothing more than a forgone conclusion to him?

"Hmmm . . ." Karine was lost in thought, her forehead wrinkled in concentration. "Ah—of course he wants to marry you . . . There had to be a reason because he has had so many women rich, poor, beautiful—all who would have gladly given anything for a proposal from him. Why you, I am asking myself. But, actually, it all fits into place."

"Karine, whatever ridiculous notion you are concocting, I will not listen to it. Lord Will may be an expert in seduction, and now he can add an expert in making marriage proposals to his list of roguish qualities—but this proposal will be his last. We plan to have a long and happy marriage together."

"Oh, I forgot. But then—you English women are determined to remain in the comfort of the dark, priding yourselves in fulfilling their husband's every whim. We French women prefer to know our demons so we can tame them to make sure they fulfill *our* every need."

Sophie sighed and shook her head. "All right Karine, I see I shall have no peace until you have your say."

Karine lifted her eyebrows and shoulders in perfect harmony. "Far be it for me to tell you how to live your life, Mademoiselle Sophie. And you have shown precious little in the way of gratitude for everything I have done for you . . ."

There was a long pause as Karine examined her apron.

Would this night ever end? But she knew if she did not listen to her devious maid, Sophie would suffer anxieties all night. "Karine, you know how much I appreciate your advice and everything you do for me."

Karine dusted the edge of the small table with her finger. "Perhaps you will show your thanks by allowing me your new rose-colored cloak?"

Sophie sighed. "Agreed."

"And the matching parasol and reticule you will never use?"

Tiredly, Sophie waved her acquiescence and lowered herself before the table and looking glass. Her haggard appearance startled her.

"Well," Karine said with a lofty tilt to her petite head, "the Mornington chits's maid told me just last week that there has been an alarming stream of males demanding interviews with Lord Will. They are those vulgar sort of men down from London," she paused and gave a sly wink. "Rosario is an adept eavesdropper, and she said that she had even overheard the men demanding vast sums of money from Lord Will, or else . . ."

"Or else what?"

"Or else, whatever," she said with her Gallic shrug. "Don't you see? He is marrying you above all those other beautiful ladies because you will be richer than anyone he knows, and he obviously needs money to pay off moneylenders *right now*. It is amazing the lengths a man will go to avoid being maimed for life."

Sophie closed her eyes and felt the embodiment of her soul drop to somewhere around her ankles. "He is a gambler then. A wastrel—*another fortune-hunter*."

"The very devil himself, if you were to ask me," Karine added for good measure. "But don't misunderstand me. You must marry him. But you must also make him well and truly fall in love with you. When you have him on the tip of your finger, you can decide what you want to do about it. I would force him to be your slave, while you dispense favors when the mood strikes you." She cocked her head to one side and looked over Sophie's physique. "Personally, I think your chances of success are about one in ten thousand, but we will at least have some fun—for once—trying. And we can leave this boring backcountry hole for the amusements of town before the sea air ruins both of our complexions."

Sophie slowly flexed her hunched shoulders back. The warmth of William's embrace had left her body, and a detached calm replaced it. She felt the first ice-cold intention to exact retribution trickle into her veins and for the first time in her life, she couldn't stop an action she knew to be sinful. Her innocence—physical and emotional—had been stripped from her quite thoroughly and heartlessly and the desire to hurt in return took root. "Oh, we'll go to London all right. But I'll not marry Lord Will."

"Are you out of your mind? Of course you will marry him. You have no choice. He ruined you— and perhaps got you with child. You'll never find a more suitable match, nor will you be able to accede to your inheritance," Karine said, then winked. "And he is an expert lover as well, don't you think?"

Sophie looked at her quickly.

"Of course, I have no personal knowledge of this. It is just that his brother was—" Karine blinked her eyes and hastily looked aside.

"No, I will not have him," Sophie said quietly. "And I am fairly sure there will be no conse-

quences to our actions of tonight. It is most likely
the wrong time if I am to believe what the midwife
in Wales told me. As to my being ruined, that will
be an obstacle, but not insurmountable. I have the
advantage that everyone already thinks I was ruined when I left London. So there'll be no awkward
scenes explaining myself to the one I do marry."
Sophie paused when she saw Karine's incredulous
expression. "No, I'll not have Lord Will no matter
what you say."

"You *are* a fool, then," Karine said. "Why do I
always have to serve the imprudent ones? I should
have been born a man so I could have been a valet.
It would have been so much more amusing, listening to their exploits and conquests than the silly
talk of love and respect I must hear from females.
Life is to be lived, mademoiselle, not frittered away
in a glass tower. Your great character will provide
cold comfort on winter nights alone in your bed."

"Karine, you misunderstood me. I did not say I
wouldn't marry. I said I would not marry that
spawn of Satan. We will leave for London, and I'll
marry a member of the *ton,* and I'll inherit my
fortune. I'll also become known as the most sought
after, extremely eligible, soon-to-be heiress in all
of London. And you'll help me. If I must marry, it
will not be to a lying, cheating fortune hunter, but
to an honest fortune hunter in the worst case
scenario—or to an intelligent, kind, caring aristocrat who has little need of my riches in the best
case. And I'll make Lord Will rue the day he
thought I could so easily be gulled."

"Well, as long as we return to London, and it
necessitates a lot more shopping, which your plan
will, and you promise to take my advice more seri-

ously, for I've a reputation to maintain"—and here she sniffed—"then perhaps I'll go along with your arrangement." Karine's outrageous behavior explored new heights.

Unfortunately, her maid also had a sense of fashion and style that was unparalleled, and Sophie would need Karine if she was to have any chance of attaining success.

Sophie did not say it, but one day she also hoped to surprise Karine by her London conquests so much so that the ridiculous maid would literally swoon and grovel her praises. Sophie smiled in bitterness. Well, perhaps she might be successful in her retaliation of that lying, scoundrel Lord Will, by living a phenomenal life, but it was doubtful she would ever wring a word of praise from that petite loaf of a French maid. One must be realistic, after all.

Will lay back in the warm soapy bathwater and rested his head on the edge of the copper tub. There was a suggestion of a smile about the corners of his mouth as he closed his eyes.

He felt as satisfied as a well-fed wolf in his lair.

He had left her reluctantly last night. Her gown had to be repositioned and her hair repinned. But when he had departed at the doorway leading from the music room to the terrace, he had promised, in the most enticing and amusing language, to return to her the next day. He had gone so far as to name the time and she had laughed but had not said no. He'd also suggested they be married by special license because she could very well find herself in an interesting condition with unamusing speculation from the beau monde.

William smiled again. The possibility of a child. His child. He almost laughed. By God, he had never imagined it.

He could not believe his good fortune. Little had he envisioned two weeks ago finding perfect happiness in this little piece of England on the edge of nowhere. And suddenly, he felt strangely detached—as if everything had happened too quickly, too perfectly to be real. But this tall, bonny Welsh bride was his and they would be wed as soon as possible.

There was only the slightest twinge of guilt over his joy in her money. He tried to ignore it.

William opened his eyes at the sound of Jack Farquhar carrying in a steaming pitcher of water. He leaned forward to receive the water on his soapy head.

"Why, do my eyes deceive me? Do I detect a familiar self-satisfied contentment in the air? Or did you just over imbibe last night and the effects have not worn off?" Jack busied himself about the chamber, laying out clothes that he had carried in with him, sharpening the edge of the razor with a strop.

Will exited the bath and accepted the towels from his valet who then retrieved a sealed letter from his pocket. Jack passed the note beneath his nose. "Mmmm . . . roses. Not very original, but very nice indeed. I see you have her writing love notes to you already. Fast lot those Welsh."

Will laughed. "Now, now, I can't have you besmirching the good name of the future Duchess of Cornwallis. It would behoove you to get into her good graces." He chuckled at his double entendre.

Jack's jaw dropped.

"Watch it, old man. You'll catch flies standing about in that manner," Will continued.

"The poor thing. I actually liked this one," Jack said, resuming his activities. The valet sat near Will to brush lather onto his face. "Well, that's a record. You've bedded her in less than a fortnight."

"It wasn't all that difficult, especially when you offer an irresistible proposal." Will felt slightly sick bantering about with Jack in his usual nonchalant fashion when he felt anything but. But he knew Jack would burst out laughing if he acted as seriously happy as he felt.

"It must have been the fan. It works every time." Jack began scraping the whiskers from Will's face. "So you're actually going to take on the shackle for this one? Willingly?"

"Don't be so shocked. It was bound to happen sooner or later. And by the by, I like her too."

"You're a cheeky devil. You're in it for the fortune. You can't fool me." The valet shaved the neck area.

"As I treasure my life, I'll not say another word while you hold that razor."

Jack laughed and finished the job. He dried Will's face, and turned to retrieve a cravat while Will toweled off and buttoned his shirt.

"Congratulate me, Jack, or perhaps offer me your condolences, if you prefer, for I have followed the legions of men before me and have finally found happiness in the hands of a good woman."

"A rich woman."

"Good and rich," replied Will, cocking a brow.

"Well, at least this will satisfy that nasty little man, Mr. Derby," Jack replied. "I must say, I am tired of the sight of him."

"Well, you should prepare yourself to see a good deal more of him if I am to succeed in this venture, which is precisely what I plan to do."

"Why you have to muddy yourself in *commerce*—"

"By the by, have you put together the list of nobility, military and gentry I'll approach in short order? The future patrons?"

"I think I might have found the time between cleaning your salty boots and ironing your—"

"Enough, Jack. Let us see the letter, now."

Will accepted the rose-scented missive and was surprised by its odd shape and outer paper. He tore off the thick wrapping and a small object fell onto the blue and gold Aubusson carpet.

His heart skipped a beat. The sapphire and diamond ring lay just beyond his reach, gleaming before him. He wondered if he was going to be ill. He felt paralyzed.

Jack scooped up the ring and studied it. "So she accepted you, did she?" There was a cynical gleam in his eyes.

"Don't say another word, *mon vieux*. Get out of here if you know what's good for you."

Jack placed the ring on the table nearby and shook his head. "I've never known what's good for me."

Will heard not a word. His hand shook as he read the letter.

Dear Lord William,

Thank you for the *pleasant* evening last night. I enjoyed your performance immensely on so many levels. I particularly take pleasure in an experience such as the one we shared when a gentleman can act so well the part of a besotted fiancé. But all playacting must come to an end at some point, and I do fear you forgot, in your exuberance, a most impor-

tant prop from the excellent betrothal scene.
I enclose it for your future use.

I do hope I am not leaving you at loose
ends. This was just an amusing interlude, was
it not? However, if reports are true, and you
are in dire need of funds to preserve the safety
of your person, I feel obligated *as a friend* to
tell you that there is another possibility for
your consideration. The just-widowed heiress
of the Marquis of Heathern might be an excellent candidate for satisfying your pressing ob-
ligations. Of course, there is the disadvantage
that she is staring eighty in the face, although
knowing your—shall we say—*calculating* nature, perhaps you may be willing to risk the
odds that she will not survive much past the
wedding night.

I wish you much joy, then, Lord William,
in your forthcoming nuptials. And I must
thank you for the education of a lifetime. I
only add, may God have mercy on your soul.
                    Sophie Somerset

William released all the air that he had held
trapped involuntarily in his lungs. He squeezed his
eyes shut, trying to still the wild madness swirling
in his mind.

"Do I detect a rebuff?" asked Jack.

Silence.

"By Jove, that's a first. My, but the Welsh female
has grown in my estimation—by leaps and
bounds," Jack continued.

Silence.

"That bad, is it, then?" Jack said, rising from his
seat. "I'll get the brandy."

"No," Will said, finally speaking. He could feel

his outstretched hand shaking. "Arrange for my horse to be saddled."

"Don't you think you should let a little time—"

Will's door opened without warning and Charles Mornington entered, a dazed, pale look on his face. He held a note in his hand. "They've left. Miss Owen and Miss Somerset have left." He refocused his attention on his friend. "By God, if you have had something to do with this, I'll wring your neck, I will. I am sick and tired of your antics, Will. You should have stopped your larking about years ago. Now you're just a lecherous old fool."

"Where?" Will said, quietly but with menace.

"What?" said Mornington.

"Where have they gone?"

"I'll not tell you. I'll not let you near them."

Farquhar stepped in. "Oh, go ahead and tell him. Can't you see he's gone and fallen in love with her? And it is painfully clear that you are suffering from the same ridiculous condition." Farquhar began picking up the discarded nightclothes and headed toward the door. "Now let us get a move on to town, directly. For you don't have to tell me where they've gone, or what they'll do. Let's hope by the time we get there that I'll have talked some sense into one, if not both, of you."

Jack disappeared into the hallway to retrieve the trunks and talked to himself under his breath. "Like I always say, 'Ladies—can't live with them, *can live without them*.' But do they listen?" He cackled to himself and began quietly singing one of his new favorite tunes. "Yankee Doodle keep it up, Yankee Doodle dandy. Mind the music and the step and with the girls be handy . . ."

Chapter Eight

*I*t was late to be rejoining the Season in town. But there were advantages to reentering the swirl of society at the height of the bloom and bustle. Relatively new faces were always sought after in the glittering ballrooms such as this one in the Earl and Countess of Mayne's mansion. And faces such as Sophie's, with the taint of recent scandal, were especially desirable. For everyone who was anyone delighted in following the potential for more gossip.

Sophie glanced down at her bodice. Delicate lace rimmed the edges of the ice blue ball gown. It was her favorite. She examined the display of bosom Mademoiselle Karine had suspended with a most inventive style from the new mantua-maker on Bond Street. Gone were the days when Sophie hunched her shoulders. Now she stretched her neck and displayed her shoulders and form proudly. It was a profound change.

It was only after learning of William's fortune-hunting schemes, and the resulting fury that fueled her new plan, that she had ruthlessly learned how to use her voluptuous charms to her benefit. Now every gentleman in London from the age of six and

ten to six and eighty had a flicker of interest in his
eye when he greeted her. Gone were the furtive
glances at her covered bulk. Somehow, her proud
stature and newfound confidence naturally repelled
vulgar glances and comments. In four short weeks,
she had gained a hard-won acceptance by the *ton,*
if the invitations piled on her aunt's desk were
any indication.

And tonight she was determined to make her
choice, and bask in the radiance of her success. She
only wished *he* were here to witness her ultimate
triumph in the face of the almost insurmountable
odds that she had encountered upon her return.

"My dear Miss Somerset, don't break my heart
by refusing me the next set." Lord Drummond
inched his way forward through the throng of gentlemen surrounding Sophie.

She tilted her head and fluttered her fan at the
precise pace to indicate indecision. Her eyes spar-
kling, from the reflection of the many candles be-
decking a chandelier, revealed her intention.

A chorus of protests broke out among her court
of admirers.

"Her card is full," the Marquis of Dalrymple
said, much annoyed.

"She hasn't received permission to waltz, Drummond," Mr. Hornsby continued.

"Hear, hear!" seconded three more gentlemen.

Sophie snapped her fan closed and cleared her
throat. "Why, Lord Drummond, I had not thought
to see you tonight. Most of the more, shall we say,
refined guests arrived hours ago."

"My dear Miss Somerset," Lord Drummond replied with a grin, "I was detained by my efforts to
compose a suitable verse describing your lips, your
eyes, your very soul."

"Oh, I say, most unfair," complained the Duke of Isleton.

"I see. And?" Sophie affected a haughty ennui, plying her newfound role with expertise.

"And I would request the pleasure of dancing this waltz so I can litter your person with a plethora of pithy adjectives," replied Lord Drummond.

Much as she had become adept at composing her every emotion, Sophie could not swallow the gurgle of laughter that escaped her. "Ah, well, we cannot have the verse molder so long that you begin to insert adverbs, now can we?" She tapped her fan lightly on his chest. "I accept."

Unhappy male voices followed the pair when Sophie placed her gloved hand on the proffered arm of Lord Drummond and they wove into the bevy of couples flocking onto the ballroom floor.

Sophie looked into the blue eyes of Lord Drummond as he splayed his hand on her back, and accepted her hand in his other. He was her exact height and age and his light brown hair was only a shade away from her dark blond locks. He was most adept at amusing her and had been trying to tempt her for the last month.

Lord Drummond was droll on occasion to be sure. If only he had the intense intelligence in his expression like . . . Sophie shook her head, willing her memories to disappear.

"I see you are intent on completely ruining the last shreds of my reputation, my lord," Sophie said.

"Ah, but it is part of my plan, Miss Somerset," he replied with an open countenance. "If it is wholly in tatters you'll be left no choice but to accept my proposal of marriage."

"Well, it has not escaped my notice that you've been, let us say, most *diligent* this past week in your efforts to tarnish my character," Sophie said. "I would call you a blackguard, sir, if your efforts had not failed in an extraordinary fashion. In fact, I do believe I owe you my thanks."

He sighed in mock despair. "I suspected as much. I'm afraid I was three sheets to the wind when I did it. How many gentlemen have tried to kiss you in the past week?"

"Ah, a lady does not reveal all, sir."

Lord Drummond waltzed Sophie past a pair of potted palms, through one set of doors to the terrace beyond. He had the distinct look of a male poised to steal a kiss—the same look Lord Coddington had on his face earlier in the Season.

Sophie arched a brow and deftly steered them back through the second set of doors. "My, my, Lord Drummond, I think you have had altogether too much of that, don't you agree? You assume too much," she said, laughing. "Especially before you have uttered even one line of the promised verse."

Lord Drummond accepted defeat without much grace. "My dear, I can't get our embrace from my mind. The touch of your hands in my hair, your sweet lips, and what you did to my ear, and, and"— he stared down at her décolleté—"well, you simply have the most beautiful, divine *presence* that is perfection personified."

Sophie delicately licked her upper lip and smiled.

Lord Drummond's step faltered momentarily and a sheen of perspiration appeared on his brow. "Right. Now let's see, a poem. Right."

He was concentrating. "There once was a girl from Wales, who was certainly not covered in scales. She kissed like a siren, danced like a fairy and frustrated all the poor boys to wails."

Sophie laughed.

"I do believe I forgot the line about 'the lady's tall tales.' Yes, I am certain." He had a comical expression on his face.

Lord Drummond really did possess most everything she had been looking for—wit, good looks, and most amazing of all, he was rich. She had had three sources confirm the last point before setting one of her slippers in his carriage bound for a tour of Hyde Park during the social hour.

And he was completely entranced by her carefully constructed façade—the unattainable and mysterious lady she and Karine had painstakingly created over the last few weeks.

There was no reason not to accept him. None at all.

"Have I earned my reward then?" he asked, hope shining in his eyes.

"Undoubtedly," she replied.

"Righto then. Back to the terrace."

The music ceased, and Lord Drummond looked at her. "You knew it was ending?"

She smiled and winked at him. "Your reward was the waltz, and well you know it, sir. Lead me to my aunt, will you? I fear from the look on her face I shall be departing shortly."

And then she saw him as she scanned the room for her party. *William*. Her gaze darted back. There was no one there—just like last week at the theater. But she was sure he had been partially visible, standing outside one of the doors to the terrace. Her heart plummeted.

She suddenly felt exhausted from the effort of embodying her new persona. The concentration required to enact the bold pretense of wit, charm and beauty was an unbelievable strain.

Sophie and Lord Drummond made their way toward the disapproving gaze and tight smile of Aunt Rutledge, her companion Mrs. Crosby and cousin Mari. A word or two later and the females had agreed to depart despite the pleas of Lord Drummond. Aunt Rutledge used her most haughty glare in response to the young gentleman's request to escort Sophie and a party of his making to Vauxhall two days hence.

Sophie said good-bye to her disappointed suitor and for a quarter of an hour the quartet of females was forced to wait in the great hall of the Mayfair townhouse for the arrival of their carriage. Aunt Rutledge was glowering so intently that Sophie knew better than to initiate conversation.

Sophie strolled to the gray marble full-length statue of Caesar, bedecked in nothing but laurel and grape leaves, and pondered the current state of affairs. These visions were unsettling. She supposed they were due to her refusal to see him when he had called on three separate occasions. She had not wavered. If she had, Karine would have locked her in her apartments. Her maid had wholeheartedly embraced her plan once she had seen the outrageous amount of shopping it had entailed and the inevitable castoffs.

Sophie had to be careful exiting her Aunt's townhouse. She rushed into carriages, went to small affairs where she knew the guest list in advance and ruthlessly interrupted Mr. Mornington's stuttering pleas on behalf of that, that poor excuse of a gentleman.

Every day that passed solidified Sophie's anger at William's deception. She had gained proof of his fiscal woes when she had attended a glittering *ton* event in one of the most beautiful, opulent mansions in Mayfair the first week of her return. She had overheard two elderly gentlemen tut-tutting about its forced sale.

"Shocking, Winthrop, shocking, indeed," said one.

"Poor lads of Granville had no choice but to sell this place—the marquis has not reappeared and it's been what? years, I tell you."

"I hear tell the marquis was last seen in France—in that devil Boney's court no less."

"Well, at least we still have his magnificent pile to enjoy. Our hosts have dusted it off quite nicely."

Yes, it was painfully clear to Sophie that he had never cared two straws for her—only for her inheritance, otherwise he would have found a way, despite her refusal to see him, to throw himself prostrate on his knees to beg her forgiveness. And the angrier she became, the more brittle and thick the shell in which she had encased herself grew. She would never, ever, open herself to heartbreak again.

She knew the game well now. She had learned it from the best. And Karine had furthered her education. Uninterest, feigned or—much better—real, was the most potent aphrodisiac in the *ton*. She had become adept at her façade. Sophie had become archly unattainable and had maintained a mysterious air that drove gentlemen to distraction.

The one trait Sophie possessed that Karine had been unable to filter from her was her inherent compassionate nature. It was the ingredient that made her different from the other more haughty, selfish and jaded females. Within days the gentlemen of London had risen uniformly in a fevered pitch of interest, jockeying for position at each event she attended.

There was only one reason she was willing to put herself through the rigors of a London courtship instead of tromping back to Porthcall, whose distant, haunting past beckoned her in her dreams. After her initial burst of anger had cooled, she thought about the people she loved and who loved her—Aunt Rutledge, Mari and a scattering of her mother's relatives in Wales, as well as some of the people in Burnham-by-the-Sea.

After seeing the good she had been able to wrought in Burnham with her contributions to the school, the poor and the infirm combined with the opportunity of securing a wonderful spouse for Mari as well as possibly some, if not all, of her Welsh cousins, Sophie knew in her heart and her mind, that she could not pass up this chance to help so many of her own.

Perhaps her initial plan to return to London had been borne by a stinging desire to retaliate in kind to Lord Will. But now it had grown into so much more. She realized that she had been cowardly and selfish when she had refused to heed Mari's arguments last spring. Then, she had been a pious spinster, unsure of herself and in possession of a dreadful trusting nature. The solitary life of a recluse, without familial or societal burdens, had proved too tempting. Now she was a fully grown woman and as such could not evade the responsibilities to her family.

Sophie was roused from her thoughts by the signal of a footman. Within moments, she, along with Aunt Rutledge, Mrs. Crosby and Mari, was bustled into the dark blue lacquered closed carriage with the gold ornate Cornwallis "C" emblazoned on each side. The door latch had not even caught before Aunt Rutledge let loose her displeasure.

"Really, Sophie, you have been here for less than a month, and I don't know whether I should congratulate you on your successes or be thoroughly put out." Her old aunt's plumage was shaking mightily. "Tonight's ball was a classic example. I thought I might expire when I saw you waltzing with Lord Drummond. The look on Sally Jersey's face—well, you may be assured your name will never cross the patronesses' collective lips along with any compliments."

Mrs. Crosby waved a perfumed handkerchief in front of Aunt Rutledge's nose.

"Thank you kindly, Gladys."

Sophie sighed. "At nine and twenty I should not have to seek permission to waltz and besides, I thought you would be pleased by all the attention, Aunt." Sophie looked for support from Mari and her aunt's companion, Mrs. Crosby, a distant cousin of the same age as the dowager who was indebted to her grand cousin for taking her in.

Mrs. Crosby said nothing, preferring to concentrate on the carriage lamp.

Sophie widened her eyes and made an encouraging motion to Mari.

"Well," Mari interjected softly, "you must agree that Sophie has been successful at attracting a few admirers. Was that not the point of returning here? I would not listen to the old biddies."

"I beg your pardon?" Aunt Rutledge huffed. "I am one of those old biddies you speak of! And twelve suitors is not my idea of a few." She turned to Sophie. "Your character is being called into question, gel, and yet you sit there cool as can be with that odious cat-in-the-cream-pot expression you have so recently acquired. What can you be thinking?"

Sophie had learned that her aunt pretended a ferociousness that she rarely, in truth, embodied. In fact, Sophie sometimes believed that her aunt delighted in this marrying business more than any of them. "Everything is going better than I had hoped, Aunt. Was it not a stroke of good luck that wager Lord Drummond put in the betting books at his club? I am much obliged to him and shall remember to ask my future husband to make a toast to him during the wedding breakfast."

A strange sound came from the corner. Sophie saw that it was Mrs. Crosby attempting to stifle a giggle.

"Gladys," Aunt Rutledge said, "don't encourage her. And you, missy"—she turned to Sophie—"are treading on remarkably thin ice. I find nothing amusing, whatsoever, about the audacious antics of that Drummond boy. He opened you and other ladies up to being accosted by every member of White's. Honestly . . . wagering that you had the most—what was it?"

"Arousing kiss," the three ladies answered simultaneously.

"That was it. *Most arousing kiss in London.* Give me my smelling salts, Gladys. And now all my acquaintances are furious, saying that every gentleman in town is trying to find a lady who, who can— Oh, heaven forbid! I can't believe I have been put in the position to discuss this most vulgar topic. Why in my day, a young lady—"

"Yes, I know, Aunt Rutledge. I am sorry. But Lord Drummond's actions are not my fault."

"Well, I say it is your fault that the ladies of good *ton* are all in danger of being mauled behind every hothouse bit of shrubbery at evening entertainments. And you, gel, are those young bucks' primary target—for comparison purposes apparently. Really, Sophie!"

Sophie swallowed her smile. "Oh, Aunt Rutledge, you know that isn't true. And besides, I think most of the young ladies and old are secretly delighted to have an eligible gentleman give them a chaste kiss. It might even give the mothers a chance to force those selfsame young bucks into making an offer. They should thank me." Sophie yawned and leaned back into the well-padded squabs of the carriage, finally releasing all the tension in her back.

Mari shook her head. "The transformation is complete. Your father is turning in his grave."

Aunt Rutledge pushed away the smelling salts Mrs. Crosby had placed under her nose. "They are calling you the Hoyden Heiress in earnest now. And I'm afraid I am going to have to withdraw my support for your inheritance as I do not see how you will be able to secure a proper match. If only you had accepted Lord Coddington. He was everything proper and charming. But, I promised not to— Never mind. Now then, where was I? Yes, I promised my brother I would not sign the papers granting you the title and the inheritance unless you married a gentleman of good *ton* capable of guiding you to ensure the proper continuance of the dukedom. I fear I will be forced—"

"I have had four offers from acceptable gentlemen in the last week," Sophie said quietly. She examined the extremely low bodice of her evening gown, and lowered the lace a fraction more.

"What!" the three ladies cried. Mrs. Crosby dropped the smelling salts and Mari lowered a handkerchief she had raised to her face.

"Four offers. One from Mr. Hornsby over aspar-

agus and aspic, following tonight's supper dance,
one from Lord Drummond, in Hyde Park last
week, of course. Then there was the offer from His
Grace, the Duke of Isleton, but that one is out of
the question. I refuse to marry a gentleman seven
years younger than I. The final offer came from
that Marquis . . . Dalrymple. I told him I would
take his offer under consideration but I think I'll
not have him even though he is kind and I dare
not hurt his feelings. His expression reminds me
too much of a hound and his embrace left me feeling rather . . . pawed over."

"Outrageous. You are beyond the pale and completely lacking the moral fiber required of a
duchess."

"I do beg your pardon, Aunt." Sophie unconsciously curled her aching toes in her dancing slippers. "But I thought a bit of plain speaking,
between family only of course, was in order. And
since I agreed to offer myself to the most eligible
gentleman in exchange for the full-to-bursting cof-
fers of Cornwallis, I thought I should tell you how
the game stands. I know how important an heir to
the dukedom is to you, and I want to please you,
Aunt Rutledge. I will of course accept the marquis,
or Lord Drummond if I cannot find a better aspi-
rant by the end of the Season. Oh, I almost forgot.
Lord Coddington renewed his acquaintance with
me too, tonight, although he cannot compete with
the other two gentlemen. Do you agree, Aunt
Rutledge?"

Sophie glanced at her aunt whose countenance
had gone from red to white in moments. Aunt Rutledge hemmed and hawed and finally spoke. "Well,
now that you mention it, I have always thought
Lionel Coddington would be an eminently perfect

match for you. Our family has known his for many
years and his character is without blemish. If you
accept his suit, I shall sign the papers immediately
and we can end this horrid search. And if we are
diligent enough, we should be able to put everything to rights." Aunt Rutledge picked up one of
Sophie's hands and patted it. "You know, my dear,
I worry my health is in decline. And it is my dearest
wish to see my brother's affairs all settled before I
depart this mortal coil."

"You trust and like Lord Coddington very much,
do you, Aunt? This would make you happy? I long
to make you happy." Sophie released her aunt's
hands and pulled the ends of her silk shawl tighter.
"I suppose we would rub along together as well as
most of the husbands and wives of the aristocracy."

"And what is more," Aunt Rutledge continued
with more vigor, "he knows the Cornwallis properties and would surely do well by them. Visited them
many a time with his father over the years. Oh,
Sophie, I know he will make you happy. You must
trust my instincts."

Sophie sighed. "Would you mind very much if I
put off my decision for the moment, Aunt? I promise to think carefully about what you have said.
Lord Coddington has not actually made me another
formal offer, yet."

Out of the corner of her eye, Sophie saw Mrs.
Crosby nudge Aunt Rutledge.

"Oh, yes, my dear, Sophie. I would not force this
on you. Let us wait to see how it goes. I only ask
you to consider him in the best possible light. And,
my dear, do take better care in future. I'm mortally
tired of hearing your name on every gossip's lips."

Aunt Rutledge looked as if she was about to
continue her admonishments but the abrupt halt of

the carriage forbade it. The gloved hand of a servant reached into the carriage and Sophie, who was closest to the door, followed by Mari, descended from the carriage.

Gladys Crosby placed a staying hand on her cousin when Agnes Rutledge moved her plumed bulk across the carriage's bench in anticipation of the servant's hand. "You should be ashamed of yourself, Agnes. Trying to force Coddington down her throat when she has two eminently desirable offers. She has no interest whatsoever in the boy."

Agnes Somerset Rutledge, the elder—by fifteen years—and only sister of the recently deceased Duke of Cornwallis, made defensive sounds.

"You think I don't know what you're about?" asked Gladys. "Well, I won't allow you to force her to marry the son of the man you still pine for. It is patently evident to me you hope to live vicariously through your niece. Shame on you. No one else has the nerve to stand up to you. And I don't care if you send me away for forcing you to hear the truth of the matter."

Gladys accepted the hand of the servant before Agnes because her cousin had been rendered motionless in her shock. For the first time in her life Gladys Crosby felt the thrill of speaking her mind. She was equally sure she would awaken in the morning in horror of her actions, and be forced to swallow her pride and beg forgiveness. But she could savor her small heroics the rest of the night.

Chapter Nine

The wind rushed through William's hair during his ride at dawn along a muddy track among the low marshes and ditches of Battersea Fields. He knew better than to risk the remote chance that one of the three male Tolworths trolling London would take it upon themselves to search Hyde Park's infamous Rotten Row. He cursed the Tolworths and his ill luck and urged his mount to a breakneck pace.

The varying green shades of summer foliage flashed through the gray mist at a dizzying speed. It failed to bring him a moment's cessation of his constant thoughts of her. *Sophie.* Damn her goodness, her kindness, her Venus-like self. If it had only been a matter of his physically still wanting her. That would be eminently curable. In fact, he knew of a certain lush actress at Drury Lane who would satisfy his every— The image of Sophie's gentle eyes, encouraging him to take her innocence that night in the music room, flooded his mind. He suddenly experienced the same gut-wrenching sensation that had been torturing his thoughts and dreams since last he saw her.

He came to an abrupt stop then allowed his

horse to walk off his exertion. Steam from the horse's flanks rose to mingle with the mist. William dropped the reins at the horse's withers and took great gulps of air.

He must get her alone tomorrow. All his previous efforts had failed. He had never met with such a run of ill luck. She had refused his calls, which was not surprising, he supposed. But she had also been ruthless in her endeavors to evade any possibility of seeing him—on the street, in the park, even in church she had surrounded herself with a clutch of females and increasingly with a band of besotted gentlemen. It was the latter that perturbed him the most.

William thought about what he would do to Drummond if he ever came face-to-face with the peer. He felt violently ill at the thought of that lapdog having the audacity to kiss his Sophie. Last night had been the worst. Watching the pompous twit waltzing with Sophie in his arms had unleashed a fury he had never known. If Mornington had not been there to bash some sense in him he would have created a scene in the Mayne's ballroom that would have been talked about for the next century.

William supposed it was a good thing that Mr. Derby, the architect, and now Mr. Baird, the man Will had employed to oversee construction consumed so many of his hours each day. They were making genuine progress ever since his spectacular win at a gaming hell a fortnight ago. This would hold off the creditors for at least another month. But he must raise more funds, and it was horrendously difficult to secure an audience with possible investors when he was in hiding.

The intelligence of his original idea of creating a

new banking institution with progressive ideas about investments and credit was losing, in his more desperate, darker days, some of its brilliance. If he had not already invested so much time and effort into his dream of restoring his family's name and properties, he had to concede that he might have chosen a simpler method. But simplicity had never been his strong point. And damn it all, his idea was sound and it would be a boon to so many, notwithstanding his primary goal of reestablishing himself and his brother.

William reached the end of the track and pulled his pocket watch from its resting place. Noting that he had but five minutes before he was due to meet Jack and Mornington at a costumer's, he urged his mount into a slow trot across Parkgate Road. The shop owner had accepted a significant monetary incentive from Mornington to open his shop early for a clandestine viewing of his wares.

A man wearing a vibrant yellow waistcoat surrounded by a robin's egg blue coat loomed up ahead. A bark and a hiss confirmed William's guess and he shook his head. A commotion was in progress. Blending in with a crowd had never been Jack Farquhar's forte.

"Now, now, Mrs. Tickle. Mustn't tangle with the shop's mouser, my love," Jack said when William arrived. "Now, my good man, if you would just let us into your delightful establishment, I'm sure we can come to some sort of an arrangement about my dog." He turned his head and whispered loudly to Mornington. "Give him a few more quid, if you please."

William plucked Mrs. Tickle's leash from Jack's hand and gave it and his horse's reins to an aproned assistant shopkeep nearby. A coin and a word directed the man to walk the horse and the dog.

"Well, I never—" Jack crossed his arms before William hustled him into the shop, Mornington's stout form skulking in behind them all.

"I know you never. Come on, then, let's collect our costumes before the rest of Mayfair arrives," interrupted William.

"But we need to outfit Mrs. Tickle too."

"All in good time. Now, sir"—William turned to the shop owner—"will you be so kind as to show us various costumes from say, two or three decades ago?"

"Oh goody," said Jack, quick to reapply his smile. "I do so love wigs, and powder. Oh, and patches, and higher heels, and those divine cosmetics."

The shopkeeper looked over Jack and sized him up in an instant. Without batting an eye, he turned to enter the back of the shop. "Let's start with hoops and panniers for you, *madam*."

Mornington and William burst out laughing.

Jack sniffed. "Well, I don't see anything remotely funny—"

"Mr. Charles Mornington, lately of Burnham-by-the-Sea and"—the Master of Ceremonies leaned in close to Mornington—"and?" he repeated.

Charles whispered something into the man's ear.

"And Lady *Jacqueline* and Mr. Barclay," the man announced to the ballroom full of people who turned to catch sight of the late arrivals.

"Thank you, my good man," Jack said in a high voice. Will's erstwhile valet dazzled the lorgnette-clinging crowd in his high-necked, gold-colored gown with six-foot wide panniers and enough white powder on his face and hair to look like the queen of the dead. Only the bright red lips and quivering heart-shaped patch near his left eye proclaimed he was, indeed, alive.

The Master of Ceremonies' eyebrows rose three notches after noticing Mrs. Tickle, wearing a miniature court-jester costume complete with a hat, tucked firmly against Jack's bodice.

"Stop gripping my arm, you imbecile," Mornington hissed at Jack.

"The better to make sure you don't escape, my dear," Jack replied under his breath.

"You owe me, Will. You owe me," Mornington sputtered.

William looked through the dark eyeholes of his mask, which covered all but his lips. His simple black domino and hat hid his identity and the stark evening clothes beneath. "Did I not promise to repay you in spades? With Miss Mari Owen's hand, no less."

"Yes, but, I fail to see how—"

"Keep smiling, now. The hosts are at twelve o'clock," Will gritted out while he smiled.

They scraped and bowed and did their duty to their hosts. And the countess was so taken with Mrs. Tickle that she didn't notice Lady Jacqueline's faint shadow of a beard.

"Do you see them?" Mornington leaned up to William to capture his attention.

"No. It's next to impossible to make anyone out in all this court dress. There are more gray wigs here than when Prinny visits Parliament," William replied, half hiding behind a gray marble column.

Jack turned to Mornington. "Would you be a dear and fetch me and Mrs. Tickle a little something to wet our throats? Hmmm? Or perhaps a little dancing first? I long for a waltz, don't you, Mr. Mornington?"

Mornington, flustered and red in the face, replied, "I think not." He plastered a smile on his face and bowed as a dowager duchess passed and nodded to him.

"Why, I do declare," Jack continued, staring at a couple waltzing. "I should have opted for male attire, after all, if they're going to allow that sort of thing. How very liberal our good hosts are in their way of thinking."

William stared at the dancing couple. The taller figure was a gentleman clad in full court dress, only a mask obscured his face. He held in his arms another gentleman—or no. William squinted. It was a person dressed in similar clothes, complete with a powdered gentleman's wig. *A tall, voluptuous figure.* At that moment, the figure tilted its head and laughed, in a gloriously warm, utterly feminine fashion.

William's gut clenched along with his hands.

He forced his gaze toward the circle of people surrounding the dancers and spotted the aunt and Miss Owens. "All right Mornington, here's your chance, man. Dance with Jacqueline here and show us some teeth. In front of the object of your affection, if you please. Then ask Miss Owens for the supper dance. I shall think you a complete dolt if you are unable to whisk her away for an impassioned proposal." He pushed the couple toward the dance floor, one much more willing than the other.

Jacqueline laughed, handed his pug to William and launched into an exaggerated waltz with Mornington.

William narrowed his eyes as he watched Sophie and her partner dance toward the far corner of the room. He tried to regulate his breathing. It was just a simple waltz and the gentleman was maintaining the proper distance between them. It was just the enchanted expression on Sophie's lips and her tight articles of clothing, emphasizing her every curve that aggravated him.

"For the love of God, doesn't she know there is a reason females should not show their wares so blatantly?" Will said to himself. Mrs. Tickle cocked an ear.

He forced himself to look at Mari Owens. That young lady was watching Mornington with Lady Jacqueline and fanning her face rapidly. The color had drained from her cheeks. Sophie's aunt was firmly entrenched in conversation with three older ladies.

His plan might work, but only if . . .

William scanned the dance floor. They had disappeared. He cursed to himself and stalked the outer edges of the ballroom toward the doors and the terrace beyond. The room was bursting with bejeweled members of the haut *ton* packed tighter than a tin of sardines. It was two steps forward, and one step back to avoid each paniered court gown and leaning wig.

The terrace, illuminated with colorful lanterns, was empty save for an older couple taking the air and a footman carrying a tray of canapés. William snatched one off the tray, then took the stairs two at a time down to the gently sloped garden. He paused in the shadows to allow his eyes to adjust to the darkness. Mrs. Tickle, still firmly tucked under his arm, growled.

A sensuous, throaty laugh sounded and William quickly edged the ivy covered low wall around a curve.

There, silhouetted in the moonlight, stood a pair in a classic, theatrical pose.

". . . pray don't deny me, Miss Somerset, if you will only accept me." The taller figure was moving in for the kill, lips puckered into service.

Will jiggled Mrs. Tickle, and whispered in her ear, "Get him, girl."

The pug fairly leapt from his arms and tore across the space separating them from the object of prey. Small needlelike teeth sunk into the swain's stockinged Achilles heel and the dog's jester hat swayed side to side. It was all Will could do not to give himself away in his amusement as he darted behind the nearest ancient oak.

A howl of pain erupted from the gentleman, along with concerned noises from Sophie. The man littered the air with a string of foul curses as he jangled his leg in an effort to rid himself of the pug. Mrs. Tickle eventually released him, but continued growling and snapping, forcing the man to flee in a most enjoyable, cowardly fashion toward the terrace. Not the smallest effort or word of concern for Sophie's welfare left the man's lips in his hasty retreat.

Mrs. Tickle barked once her delight, brushed her hind legs in the grass as a sign of victory and trotted to the oak tree for a reward.

William emerged from behind the tree and surreptitiously gave the canapé to the dog before facing Sophie. One look at her made him glad he had stifled the urge to chuckle. Hands on hips, legs spread wide, she looked the veritable impenetrable fortress.

"I see now why you allow your man the luxury

of a pet. How very clever and *brave* of you. And you did not even have to dirty your hands," Sophie said.

"You allowed me little choice, *chérie,* given your refusal to see me. I thought the plan moderately clever, actually. Separating a gentleman from a lady must be handled delicately." He stepped closer to her. "You should be thanking me. I exposed him for the chicken-hearted individual that he is."

"I'm sure he'll send someone out for me. You'd best be prepared to go."

"We shall see. Most men of his ilk rarely expose their weaknesses to others, especially if a lady is at stake."

"How true, Lord Will. You taught me that quite well."

William's mind raced, trying to find the words necessary to bring her about. His memorized speech fled as she lowered her mask and he gazed into her beautiful face. A patch next to her full lips glittered in the moonlight.

"Sophie, are you with child?"

"Ah, is that what this is about? No. I am sorry to snatch your last shred of hope for a most advantageous marriage. I suppose this means the Dowager Marchioness of Heathern did not accept you?"

"Sophie . . ." William closed his eyes. He had so hoped there would be a child.

"Ah, I see, no."

"Sarcasm does not become you."

"And grasping does not become you, my lord."

"Sophie," he said again, taking hold of her cold hand. She instantly retrieved her fingers from his. "I realize my motives appear suspect to you, and I should have explained it all to you sooner, but you must understand that—"

"You are a fortune hunter?" she interrupted. "Yes, I must say I never could understand why you took such pains to hide the fact from me when so many marriages involve matches much like ours would have been. But I dislike duplicity. I can forgive it once, and in your case, I did. But no one likes to be played the fool twice."

"And that is why I am here, Sophie. To apologize. Will you at least allow me that?"

Sophie looked down to find Mrs. Tickle scratching her buckled shoe. She kneeled down to gather the pug in her arms and scratch behind her ears. "I don't know."

"Then may I be allowed to explain it all to you?"

"No. I'm tired of hearing all the various reasons why gentlemen are in need of funds. But I think I will accept your apology for deceiving me. I think if only because I must thank you for teaching me more than anyone the machinations of the upper circles."

William felt wretched, watching her. She had the same cynical yet charming countenance he had caught on his face many a time. He had put that expression on a face that had only ever been open and honest in the past. He hardened himself to his resolve. He would restore her.

"And," Sophie continued, "as I am always generous when gratitude is in order, I shall offer a serious candidate to help you solve your dilemma."

"Unless you're willing to reconsider my proposal, I assure you that you will be unable to tempt me with someone else," William said.

"No, it is not I. It's Lady Mary Russell, the Earl of Shanet's daughter."

William grimaced.

"As you might have heard, she was left at the

altar a fortnight ago and the poor dear confided in me that she's in search of a fast marriage of convenience as she cannot bear the pitying looks. I think the two of you would suit. An added benefit is that you'd be forced to move to her father's estate in Surrey, well away from the lure of the vices that tempt you in town."

William knew she wouldn't believe any attempt he made to cleanse his character. In fact, she'd assume it was all a pack of lies. Unconsciously he reassumed the façade he'd taken more than two decades ago. "I suppose you've tired of the idea of wearing men's pantaloons, despite tonight's intriguing display, then? If I wed this jilted bride, this might be the last time you'd be able to wear them, my dear, in case you've forgotten." When he saw the question in her eyes he continued. "The wager. How soon they forget."

"No, I haven't forgotten wagering is of prime importance in your life. But I wouldn't be so sure of your success in this particular gamble."

A flicker of fear snaked up his spine. "You're not betrothed, Sophie, are you?"

She looked straight at him through half-shuttered eyes. A look that filled him with grief anew, so much did it look like a mirror of himself.

"Why, yes. Yes, I am, most assuredly." She wore a half smile on her lips.

"To whom?" he whispered.

He finally forced her to break contact with his gaze.

"Why, I haven't decided, precisely," she replied.

He exhaled with relief. "So you've more than one prospect?"

"I thought you knew. And I shall select one by the end of the month."

"So you've not given your word." It was more of a statement than a question. "And who are the lucky bastards?"

"Now, now, my lord, such language."

"Sophie, it will not do. I shall have you in the end, my darling. I shall slay whosoever dares to assume my place. You became mine in the music room at Villa Belza."

Sophie stiffened. "You presume too much. By your reasoning a goodly portion of the women in England and France are yours as well."

If she would just allow him to hold her once again, he was confident, over time, he'd be able to convince her of his honest feelings and intentions. He must change tactics.

"Miss Somerset, you are too good. Thank you for granting me this quarter hour and your forgiveness of past events. I'll not trouble you any longer, I promise, if you'll grant me the final pleasure of a farewell kiss."

"No."

"Then a set of dances?"

A long pause heightened his hopes.

"Perhaps. But only if you promise never to seek my acquaintance again."

"Agreed." He would say whatever was necessary to get her into his arms again, fire and brimstone be damned.

Sophie handed the dog to him and walked resolutely back to the ballroom. At the last moment, Will touched her slim arm. "I shall seek you out for the next waltz."

He turned on his heel before she could respond, then went in search of Lady Jacqueline and Mornington. William discovered them cooling their heels in the front entrance hallway, their heated whispers echoing within the arches.

"What's going on here?" Will asked.

"I'm leaving, Will," Mornington said.

"Old fiddle-faddle got a mite peeved when I found myself in a most uncomfortable situation," Jack replied, lifting his chin in the air.

"And the situation was?"

"He was going to relieve himself in the ladies' withdrawing room, for Christ's sake," replied Mornington in a whisper.

Will bit back a grin.

"Thank heavens, a delightful— You would have found her amusing, I'm sure," Jack said, looking at Will through his lorgnette. "Anyway, a delightful little French maid, by the name of Mademoiselle Karine Marcher, took one look at me outside the withdrawing room and led me to a nice secluded place where I could take care of my needs. She was most entertaining. We've become the best of friends."

William blinked. "Petite, with a cynical, razor sharp wit?"

"Exactly."

"Miss Somerset's ladies' maid," William stated.

Jack clapped his hands excitedly. "How convenient. By the way, I agreed to give her a small token of appreciation, which I am sure one of you will happily supply."

Mornington sighed.

"Have you proposed to Miss Owens?" Will asked his friend.

"Absolutely not. This has been a complete unmitigated disaster between Jacqueline's *needs* and flamboyant dancing, and I haven't been able to find

Miss Owens. I think she was so crestfallen when she saw me with Jacqueline here that she disappeared."

"Come on now, back to the ballroom. I saw her and the Cornwallis relation next to the hosts just a moment ago. Time for us both to face the music," Will winked and handed Mrs. Tickle to Jack.

"And what am I to do then? I refuse to be a wallflower. A girl has to have some fun once in her life," Jack said, then looked down at his pug. "And have you had any fun, my love? I do believe you have if that"—Jack sniffed the dab of yellow on her snout—"curried egg on your nose is any indication."

The crush was miserable tonight. All the young misses must have begged their relations to accept so they could wear something besides the modest white dresses that were their badges of innocence. Why, oh, why had she agreed to a set of dances with *him*? Normally her card would've been full but her costume had worked against her in the end. Her admirers hadn't recognized her in gentleman's dress or were lost in the uproarious crowd.

She feigned interest in her aunt and Mari's less than scintillating conversation all the while considering her situation. After glancing at Mari's pallid countenance, she'd determined to ask her aunt for an early leave-taking. But Lord Coddington's father approached and preceded her request by soliciting the great lady's hand for the next set, giving rise to a giddy expression on her relation's face.

Sophie sighed. How in heaven was she to get through a waltz with William? She'd thought when she'd agreed to a set that it would be a minuet, or a country-dance, but he'd disappeared into the crowd before she could refuse.

She'd barely maintained her controlled façade in the garden. And it had almost slipped entirely when he'd taken her hand. As it stood, the only reason she was able to slip inside this caricature of feminine charm and wit extraordinaire was for the noble purpose of pleasing and aiding her family, and perhaps, just perhaps, if she was honest, it was a way to hide her hurt and mortification.

The first swelling notes of a waltz filled the air.

All thought of good deeds fled with the notion of dancing with William. A cowardly act looked tempting indeed. Maybe she would retreat to the ladies' withdrawing room and face Karine's inquisition.

Sophie turned and a hot swirl glided along her tightly corseted waist. She glanced down to see the familiar bronzed and long fingered hand she knew all too well. William pulled her against the solid wall of his chest.

Chapter Ten

"*L*ooking for an escape, *ma chérie*?" he whispered in her ear. "I'd not thought you capable of breaking your word." He gently nipped her lobe then kissed the side of her neck. His mask tickled her hairline.

She was trapped. The crowd, if anything, enlarged, making it almost impossible to move let alone put arm's-length distance between them. And amazingly, everyone was laughing and amusing themselves to such a degree that no one paid any attention to what he'd just done to her. Now Sophie understood why the high sticklers frowned upon masquerades. Camouflage encouraged the taking of liberties.

William grasped her hand and made a path through the mass of people to the dancing area. His right arm curved around her waist as he assumed the correct posture for a French waltz. He glided into the first step and suddenly Sophie forgot the rest of the people in the room, so thoroughly lost was she to anyone save William.

Sophie held her breath as the intense awareness of the raw, physical sensuality of him flowed through her in waves. She was sure he was holding her much too closely but when she looked, if anything, he was being overly correct.

Music had always been her one great delight. Sophie loved feeling the music and rhythm wash over her, become part of her. She had never encountered a powerful, brilliant partner who sensed the music as she. He led her with a strong, self-assured command, allowing her to completely trust in his mastery and lose herself to the music.

And suddenly, they were traversing the room using a thrilling series of intricate steps her aunt's short, thin dance instructor had shown her but once before. William led her into a balletic leap followed by a flowing French movement in which his hips and thighs rolled against her own in the most shockingly sensual of all the proper motions of the dance. The pallid instructor's version of the steps compared to William's was like water to chocolate, or if she was truthful, like being kissed by her cousin versus being possessed by a man.

Sophie could not tell if she was dizzy from the fast pirouettes or drunk with the power of the emotions he evoked in her breast. She had never danced with anyone like this. It was as if he had worked his way past her mind into her very soul.

As she gripped his powerfully broad back, Sophie dared to look up into his face and saw only his mysterious, serious eyes surrounded by the black mask. It was mesmerizing. Within moments the full spectrum of her many encounters with him flashed before her. She saw his glistening, hard muscles naked from the bath, his laughing eyes behind the fan, the humorous nonchalance he had displayed in his valet's clothes, his unwavering charm toward the fairer sex, and then the intensity of the depths of his pain and passion when he had possessed her.

Oh, she had been showing all the trappings of a bewitching enchantress, but she realized suddenly that she had never felt truly feminine with anyone except William.

He said not a word. His eyes and his movements spoke eloquently.

And then it was over. He was bowing over her hand, and a faint buzzing in her ears grew louder before she awoke from her trance to encounter a round of applause from the onlookers directed toward Sophie and her partner. She curtsied gracefully.

And then, just as she wondered how she would gain the courage to refuse his certain request to see her again, he was gone with only one fleeting but poignant searching look.

Sophie blessed the mass of people exiting the dance floor for blocking any steps toward him her weak side was screaming for her to make.

Lord Drummond stepped before her. "My dear Miss Somerset, allow me to lead you back to your family if I cannot persuade you to dance the next set with me?" he asked, hope filling his face.

She shook her head briefly.

"Blasted inconsiderate devil not to escort you back to your aunt, if you were to ask me."

"Yes, you are right."

"Who was he?"

"I can't say." For some reason she didn't want him or anyone to know.

Lord Drummond grumbled further. "I would have asked you to waltz earlier if I had known it was you under that costume. I've been searching for you all evening." They wedged between a circle of acquaintances to join Mari.

Sophie felt her usual gaiety slipping precariously. "Would you be so kind as to bring me some lemonade, my lord?"

"Why, of course," he said, depositing her next to Mari. "Your wish is my every command. And when I return I must be allowed to exhibit more poetry so you shall feel obliged to dance with me or at least ride with me tomorrow morning. I hear tell"—and here he winked at Mari—"that you have a heretofore unknown habit of rising with the sun to partake in most unladylike gallops in the park most mornings."

"Yes, yes. Of course, sir." Sophie was willing to say just about anything to free herself from the necessity of conversing with him or anyone. She just wanted to go home to put as much distance as possible between her and—well, *him*.

Lost in thought, Sophie barely noticed Mr. Mornington asking Mari for the next set.

William knew not how he would force an opportunity to see Sophie again, but see her he would, whether it entailed spying on her twenty-four hours of every day or storming the flock of liveried footman guarding her at her aunt's townhouse. Elation had filled him when she had responded to him within the circle of his arms. He'd seen it in the depths of her eyes. His greatest fear the past month had been that she had excised him from her heart. It would have been only natural. But, it seems his luck was returning, and he knew as any good gambler that one must press the advantage when Lady Luck rode on one's shoulder.

A quick search of the garden and outer halls did not unearth his faithful valet-cum-courtesan. At least Charles was in evidence, now dancing and soon to be wooing his ladylove on the terrace. William wandered back into the house all the while wondering if his friend would bungle the delicate mating ritual known as the marriage proposal much as he himself had done.

His search took him to the inner sanctum of the jaded gentlemen's sect, the card room. Those few who were too tired or bored to partake in the frenzied revelry of the masquerade populated the room, illuminated by a single taper within a candelabra heavily coated with wax drippings.

There, his wig tipping slightly, sat Jack on a divan, hand-feeding Mrs. Tickle from a plate of choice morsels.

William skirted the two tables of cardplayers to join his valet. He could not help but overhear the conversation coming from the nearest table of four. He recognized a blond gentleman as the lord who'd had the misfortune of wagering a certain sum against William and his brother Alex in a protracted game of whist last Season. It had been the sum that had allowed William to pursue his dream of rebuilding his family's fortune.

"Playing cards is a lot like dealing with women, don't you know?" The gentleman sneered as he rearranged his diminishing counters on the green baize table.

"Do tell, Coddington," said Lord Acton, one of the other gentlemen sprawled before the table.

"Why, usually when you pick one up, you wish you hadn't."

A round of brandy-soaked chuckles circled the close quarters.

"Take the too tall and overblown form of the infamous Miss S," Lord Coddington continued in slurred tones.

An elderly gentleman leaned forward and asked his neighbor, "Who's he referring to, now?"

"The Hoyden Heiress," the other said with a knowing look.

"She shows her mud-flat origins with her ostrich height, and vulgar actresslike physique," Coddington replied, shaking his head and reaching for a card. "I surely wish my father hadn't forced me to pick that one up. Although to be fair, I suppose I shouldn't complain. When I take her to the altar, ere long, I'll not only gain her fortune but her delightful little maid as well."

"So you've gotten past the draconian aunt and landed the big fish have you?" Coddington's contemporary, Lord Acton, leaned forward in excitement. "I'd say it's rather time to celebrate. How's about a house party on your soon-to-be Cornwallis estate instead of your standard honeymoon, man? I could round out the numbers with a few friends and we could have a rousing good game."

Coddington smirked as he dealt the cards. "That's a capital idea. But"—here he leaned forward with a shrewd look on his face—"only after I have my fun with the maid. She shall be my reward for the hours of tedium I'll be forced to endure with the Amazon slut."

If Will had had a dagger, he would have slit the man's throat faster than the conspirators he had dispatched for the English government. As it was, Will hoisted Coddington to his feet and slapped his gloves in the man's face, catching his knuckles and signet ring on the man's jaw on purpose. He grabbed Coddington's lapels and made a primitive growl, "You'll meet me on Primrose Hill tomorrow, dawn, where you might find it necessary to revise your matrimonial plans in lieu of a rendezvous with your maker."

"Ah, one of Miss Somerset's many *suitors,* I presume?" Coddington mocked. "I've sampled her wares and can't fathom what all the fuss is about. You may have her all you want after she gets an heir off me. No need to fight over her. Whom do I have the *honor* of addressing?"

The bugger's cowardly acquaintances had the good sense to depart at the first sign of discord. Only the cardplayers at the other side of the large room remained.

William gripped the man tighter. "You've less than six hours to make your peace with the world, and if I were you, I'd be less worried about my name and more concerned about choosing the method by which I'll put an end to your pathetic existence. I shall see you at dawn, sir." William spat out the last word as if poison. He released Coddington roughly.

"I rather fancy swords. Won't waste a good bullet on you, I think," replied Coddington. The blond man suddenly swiped at William's head, dislodging the mask and exposing Will's face. "Ah, why Lord William of the notorious Barclay family—of mixed blood of course. A card cheat, stealer of fortunes and now, what, a defender of trollops? I'm not surprised. One can always count on a traitorous halfbreed Frenchman to—"

His words were cut short by the abrupt scraping back of chairs at the distant table. Out of the corner of his eye, William saw the hulking forms of the three Tolworth relatives who'd been prowling London since William's escape.

Soon Will found his role reversed. The beefy

arms of Tolworth and his nephew and cousin grasped him.

Coddington laughed heartily and rearranged his neckwear. "Why, I see you have a horde of *friends* joining us this evening. How convenient."

"You've avoided your responsibilities in Yorkshire long enough Lord William, don't you think?" asked Tolworth. "If you had thought to hide from us, you misjudged the matter. If you survive our affaire of honor on the morrow, you'll be singing to the parson in Scotland in three days time."

Jack jumped up from his perch where he had been discreetly observing the events. "Why, my dear sirs, you are all mistaken. This is my husband, Viscount Gaston. We have been married these last two years and we have neither of us ever set foot in Yorkshire," Jack sniffed. "My pug would never stand the cold there."

After several seconds of silence, William shook off one of the men's arms and grasped Jack about the waist. It was an inspired risk with a huge potential for failure.

He looked at Jack with the most adoring expression he could muster. "And I would never force you into the uneven climes of the northern wilderness, my dear—but I digress. As my wife was trying to tell you, I believe you've mistaken me for my brother. He has an astonishing ability to get in the damnedest scrapes and I have the misfortune of looking remarkably like him."

"Oh no, my dear, your shoulders are ever so much broader than that scallywag's." Jack looked up at Will and fluttered his eyelashes. "But it's been such a long time since we've seen him. Why, it is above a year since you ended our connection with that blemish to our family's good name."

This was going to work. The blokes had removed their hands and one of them was even brushing the back of William's domino and retrieving his mask. He would have to buy *Jacqueline* a complete new fall wardrobe; he could see it coming.

It was worth it.

"Well, I say," Tolworth said gruffly. "I suspect apologies are in order."

William accepted the apology and the mask with good grace before spying Mornington coming their way with Miss Owens in tow. Oh dear God.

"There you are. Wish me happy! Miss Owens has done me the great honor of consenting to become my bride." He turned to Miss Owens. "Do accept their good wishes, my dear. Lord William and Farquhar played a large part in our future happiness."

William did not have to look down to know that the hands, gripping his forearms once again belonged to the Tolworth relations.

Despite the glares from *Jacqueline* and William, Mornington continued blissfully on, like a pastor in the pulpit, his audience ensured, unaware of how firmly he was sealing his friend's fate.

"I knew that dog looked familiar," said Tolworth's heir and nephew. " 'Tis the one that fancy valet of his kept. Damned mongrel ate my best shoes, he did."

William gave a significant look to Jack, a look perfected through their many years together on the spy grounds of Europe.

Jack warbled a perfect feminine laugh. "Excuse me, my good man, but my pug, a female by the way, would never, ever eat common shoes for"— he reverted to his normal voice—"she prefers her meat raw." In the pug's ear he whispered, "Get him."

Mrs. Tickle for the second time that night tasted blood.

But it was not to be. William had just enough time to signal Mornington and Miss Owens to get out before the three Tolworths tackled him and Jack. A few minutes later several burly footmen and the hosts' butler herded the entire group of gentlemen outside.

The clatter of horses' hooves and carriage wheels filled the air in front of the mansion where a goodly number of drivers and whips were passing around spirits and partaking in the general conviviality of the evening.

"We'll be escorting you back to your lodging Lord William and *Lady Jacqueline* and setting a watch on your place. For we wouldn't want you to get lost on your way to Primrose Hill tomorrow morning, would we?" Tolworth chortled with laughter.

"I shall meet you," said William, "a quarter of an hour past my appointment with Coddington, with or without your watch on my heels. I'm through protecting your neck. If you really want to allow your dear nephew an early inheritance, far be it for me to deny you."

Tolworth paled and blustered about.

"Pistols or swords?" asked William.

This could only end badly. For while there was no doubt he would nick the fool with a pistol or a blade, in his experience, it almost never ended there. There was always some hotheaded male further on down the line who would attempt to exact some form of revenge.

"Pistols," replied Tolworth. "But I'll settle for this until tomorrow."

William instinctively knew what was coming. Tolworth's fist slammed into his left cheek and eye as the stout gentleman's relations held William in their grips.

Jack flung a reticule at their loutish heads and connected with the nephew's head in fine fashion. Mrs. Tickle's snarls sounded above the jeers of the workingmen who thronged the spectacle.

"All right, man, you've had your moment of glory." William shrugged off the arms holding him and fingered his bruised face. "Tomorrow you'll have your moment to wish to hell you'd left well enough alone." William spat out a fair amount of blood and wished, not for the first time, that he had chosen to live his life in France instead of among these oh-so-noble English.

Tolworth had the temerity to call honor the deceit he had employed while attempting to foist off an ugly, stupid daughter. The French were an altogether more cunning race. Oh, they might have made the devious attempt to rid themselves of an unsightly daughter, but they would have retreated when outmaneuvered and then found new prey.

Mornington shouldered his way past the onlookers to retrieve William and Jack. The trio found Charles' carriage and headed for the Mornington townhouse, Tolworth's carriage hard on their wheels.

William, suffering from an all-consuming head and jaw ache, endured his friend's alternating exclamations of joy on his betrothal and horror over William's two affaires of honor. It effectively put an end to his heady thoughts of waltzing with Sophie.

* * *

"No, Mari, I shan't listen to you for another moment," said Sophie, attaching her veiled riding hat to her coiffure with a long jeweled hat pin. Her cousin and Karine hovered about Sophie's elegant dressing room, filled with evidence of last night's masquerade ball.

"But I promise you it's true. Charles insists Lord Will loves you." Mari twisted unmercifully a handkerchief in her hands. "Perhaps he did involve you in a deceitful manner in the beginning, but he has well and truly changed."

"Your fiancé, as fine a man as ever there was, cannot be counted on when it involves Lord William Barclay—a man who has shown he can maneuver people and events to suit his every whim," Sophie retorted. She leaned forward in her seat before the looking glass and tried to pinch some color into her cheeks. She had had less than four hours of fitful sleep after the masquerade and looked all the worse for it. Only Mari looked fresh, the excitement of her betrothal had forestalled the ravages of a sleepless night.

"But aren't you worried? Charles shielded me from the ugly scene in the card room, but I'm sure those gentlemen began brawling as soon as I was shooed away."

Sophie stood up and waved at Karine to arrange the veil over her face. "I'm not concerned or surprised in the least. Lord Will has the delightful habit of inciting anger wherever he goes."

"Well, I think," Karine said, never once minding her place, " 'tis time you made a decision to accept one of the lot of them before something goes wrong." She brushed away lint on the back of her mistress's deep green riding habit. "You've stretched your ability and mine to the limit and I see nothing but a *disastre* looming if you don't make your choice, and fast."

"She has a point, Sophie," Mari said with a worried look on her face. "Personally, I don't know how you've kept up the charade."

"And I still think you should choose Lord Will no matter what you say," Karine said with a pout.

"I agree," Mari chimed in.

"Lord Drummond would be a better choice for he, at least, is an honest man. Or I shall choose Lord Coddington to please Aunt Rutledge," Sophie said.

Karine continued. "Really, you are being so foolish, mademoiselle. It's obvious to us that Lord Will is the one you most fancy no matter what you say. And Lord knows he will be the one who will bring you the most pleasure, in and out of the bedchamber."

"Mademoiselle Karine!" Mari said in shocked awe.

"Well, it is the truth and she knows it first hand," Karine said, smugly.

Mari whirled around to confront her. "Is this true? You have been with him? Oh, Sophie, what have you done?"

"It is no one's affair but my own and it's beneath discussion by you or anyone." Sophie gave a pointed look to her maid and picked up her intricately tooled horsehair riding crop. "Now if you will excuse me, I have an appointment with Lord Drummond and my groom. If I dally any longer the sun will be up and I will have missed my chance for a secret gallop."

Sophie left the room before Mari could start a harangue on the total want of morals and propriety

Sophie had so lately adopted. She was not in the mood to agree with her cousin.

Despite the controlled front she exhibited, Sophie couldn't halt the flood of memories assaulting her senses. She had almost crumbled under his intense scrutiny while waltzing with him only a few hours ago. She was wavering, unable to tamp down the feelings that had escaped last night from the deep recesses of her heart.

She had tried so desperately to forget him, and she had failed so miserably. A familiar little voice told her that perhaps, just perhaps, he did care for her just as Mari and Mr. Mornington insisted. Another voice told her she was still the fool.

In her mind's eye, she could still see his expression as they had waltzed—intense, and filled with something indefinable. Was it love? The first voice fairly screamed "yes" in her mind, asking why she wavered. She shook her head and wondered how she would respond when his inevitable card was brought to her on a silver salver later today. She wondered if her newly minted pride would play a part in her response.

Past the long carpeted stairway, and central hall, Sophie accepted the greetings of the sleepy footmen and exited the townhouse.

It was dark and cool outside. The whirling mist enveloped her form. True to his word, Lord Drummond awaited astride his chestnut horse. Sophie's groom led two horses, a small bay gelding and large gray mare outfitted with a ladies' sidesaddle.

Within moments the groom assisted Sophie onto the mare and mounted the other. She assembled her reins and set forth up the street.

"I say, Miss Somerset, Hyde Park is this way,

don't you know?" Lord Drummond was his usual jovial self despite the early hour.

"Correct," Sophie said. "However, as we are off to Regent's Park, it is the opposite direction," she said trotting northward, not bothering to make sure both men followed her.

Lord Drummond chuckled behind her. "But, Miss Somerset, why ever are we going there? It's so much farther."

"Because I'm tired of Rotten Row and the endless stream of gentlemen trying to prove their virility."

Karine's first rule of playing the coquette was to be difficult and act on every caprice. It had proven its merits, driving hordes of gentlemen to answer her every beck and call. The deferential, good-natured girl of her past seemed a dim memory. Indeed, selfishness had proved to be an easy failing to adopt.

The pair made their way along the quiet, dark streets of Mayfair trailed by Sophie's young groom. They entered the deserted outer circle of Regent's Park and with the flick of the whip, Sophie signaled her mare into a canter, which soon became a gallop when Lord Drummond's gelding tried to catch them.

Sophie laughed and enjoyed the rush of cold air on her face. She had always loved to ride but had never had the opportunity to ride a beautiful, sure-footed creature such as this mare until coming to live with her aunt. Her father had only ever had Dobby, a two-decade-old sweetheart whose gaits could best be described as slow and uncomfortable.

The mare handily won the impromptu race ending at Macclesfield Bridge. Sophie turned her head to give Lord Drummond some good-natured ribbing before she heard a shout from the groom.

The young man pointed toward something in the misty distance in the direction of Primrose Hill across the road.

"They're dueling, miss," the groom, Jemmy, called out.

"Best if we leave in the event there's a stray bullet from those fools," Lord Drummond said. "Come on then, I'll concede your victory, my dear."

"Nonsense," Sophie said already halfway across the bridge. "Let's go see."

Lord Drummond trotted toward her. "Now really, Miss Somerset, I must insist. This is no matter for a lady. It's not at all the thing."

"I'm going," Sophie said.

"No, no. Turn around, my dear. It's an affaire of honor and ladies are not at all welcome."

"Look at it this way, my lord. Perhaps I'll faint from the blood and you'll be there to catch and revive me." She didn't tell him that there was virtually no chance of that. She had seen more blood and serious injuries than many apothecaries, as there hadn't been a doctor within sixty miles of Porthcall. Everyone had turned to her father, Sophie or the midwife when in need. Bandaging injuries was second nature. "Come along, Jemmy."

Within moments she discerned they were using swords. She galloped forward, in plain view of both duelists, praying one of her party could stop this before someone was injured or killed.

And then cold fear swept her breath away. Good God! Her heart leapt in horror. It was Lord Coddington and, of all people—*William*.

Chapter Eleven

*S*ophie unhooked her leg from the sidesaddle, jumped down and ran toward Lord Will's valet, Mr. Mornington and a stranger. Lord Drummond and Jemmy were not far behind her. Mr. Farquhar grabbed her arm as she tried to dart past, heedless of the danger.

"Hold still," commanded the valet with a seriousness she had never heard from the foppish man. Mr. Mornington grabbed her other arm to hold her back. "Don't break his concentration," whispered Mr. Farquhar harshly.

"Go right ahead, my dear." The stranger, Lord Coddington's second, chuckled as he boldly examined the length of her body. "It's in your honor, after all."

"What?" Her gaze darted to the duelists.

"Hush!" Farquhar's tone demanded obeisance.

The snick of small swords sliced through the silent, dark air. The triangular blades swirled so quickly during the thrusts and parries that they were a blur of motion. The two men exhibited sophisticated phrasing and blade work amid the clash of metal on metal.

William's proud, aristocratic stance was silhouetted against the rising sun that was beating back the mist. He held his arm in a firm balanced manner, striking at his opponent in smooth, fluid movements. Lord Coddington thrust his sword with more vigorous and active motions.

The tempo seemed to increase in time with Sophie's racing heart. Oh Lord, please don't let him die. She would promise anything, just *please*. The edges of fear and guilt crept into her breast. God was exacting justice for all her sins.

The two swords clanged together at the hilts with each man trying to outmuscle the other, and for a split second, William's gaze took in Sophie.

Lord Coddington pushed with all his weight and managed to shove William off balance, then thrust his sword point, plunging into the edge of William's waist.

Sophie's breath whooshed out of her as William staggered slightly and recovered, breathing hard. Coddington, his eyes bulging and with exuberant confidence, swung his sword wildly, grazing William's brow.

"No," hissed the valet, pushing her to the ground, out of William's line of vision.

The thin razorlike cut on his face teared scarlet and gushed down William's face, impeding his vision.

Flushed with success, Lord Coddington paused, his sword hovering indecisively for a moment. Seeing the opening, William snapped his sword forward like a sapling branch pulled back and released, piercing Coddington's chest wall.

Coddington lurched, stumbled backward, then fell to the ground.

Sophie pitched forward to her feet and ran to William.

Breathing hard, Will swiped at his bloodied face and lowered himself to the wet grass.

Sophie tumbled headlong beside him. She forced him to lie down then fumbled with his waistcoat and shirt.

"Why, *chérie,* whatever are you about?" William asked.

Sophie looked into his laughing yet exhausted eyes.

"Had I known I could earn your compassion and attention and loving care by this fashion, I would've drawn blood long ago." He chuckled before a series of coughs overwhelmed him.

Sophie examined his wound and exhaled. The sword had missed William's vitals, having gone in and out of the edge of his waist. Now it was only a question of whether the wound would fester and bring on a deadly fever.

Mr. Farquhar sat beside her and opened a brown leather bag. Sophie took a bandage from the valet's hands and insisted on binding the wound herself.

"What was this nonsense about, anyway?" Sophie asked. "Lord Coddington's friend said it had something to do with me." She glanced toward William to find his valet threading a needle to address his master's cut above the brow.

William ignored her comment, calmly directing a query to his valet instead. "Is it the eye? I can't see a blasted thing."

"No, you can't see for all the blood. Don't worry. You'll live to cock this infamous brow of yours again"—Mr. Farquhar winked at Sophie—"and only too soon, I imagine. But if I ever see you lose your concentration again, over a female no less, I'm afraid I'll be forced to tender my resignation. I simply cannot serve a gentleman half so idiotic."

"I suppose I should apologize for distracting you," Sophie said stiffly.

"Oh, no, *chérie*. I would not have had it any other way. Perhaps you should assume I sustained these wounds to make you more amenable to my plight." He smiled then grimaced when the effort caused him pain.

Farquhar rolled his eyes then tilted William's face to one side. "Keep your eye open now." He poured water over William's eye and face, displacing the blood. "Can't have you blind in the next round."

Sophie touched his bruised eye and jaw. "Your poor face . . . You have been busy," she said with a light tone, despite her fear. Then, the valet's words registered. "Next round?" Sophie turned toward Lord Coddington. That gentleman lay almost motionless on the ground, surrounded by a small group. Odd that she felt so little concern for a man she had said she might marry. In the distance, Lord Coddington lifted his head off the ground to accept a drink of water. "Why, he must be worse off than William, I am sure. There'll be no next round."

Mr. Farquhar gestured toward a willow tree, its long tendrils of leafy branches hung motionless in the still air. A group of three men and their horses stood beside it, examining something. The gentlemen looked up, as if sensing her gaze, and began collecting their affairs.

"Oh, believe me, Miss Somerset, there will be," said Mr. Farquhar. "For when it comes to dueling, our Lord Will here has a natural inclination toward inducing these nasty affairs wherever he goes."

"Farquhar," William said with an edge. He took her hand gently in his own while his valet toweled his face and began stitching the cut. "Sophie, my darling, you must go. It's getting light, and there may be other witnesses. You cannot let your name be sullied further by association."

He moved his index finger to her mouth to quell her arguments. His expression was as serious as she had ever seen it. He winced with each stitch to his brow. "Go. I shall come to you very soon and then—well, we'll talk of the future." He stilled her lips again. "I promise to come directly."

His gaze transferred to a small thick glass Mr. Farquhar held, filled, quite obviously, with spirits.

"For the pain," the valet ordered dispassionately. "And to regain your nerve."

William rose with their help and tossed back the contents of the glass. "Now go, Sophie."

Sophie shook her head slowly and Mr. Farquhar made a sound of annoyance.

The group from the tree strode toward them. Mr. Mornington, Lord Drummond and Jemmy joined them.

The largest, and eldest, of the strangers addressed William. "You're not going to try and cry off, are you?" the man asked gruffly. Sophie had the strangest sensation he wanted William to answer in the affirmative.

There was an awful pause. "As a matter of fact, sir," Sophie interjected, "I'll not let anyone fight in my honor. I refuse to allow a senseless spectacle over a pointless cause."

The man looked at her brazenly. "Well, you're a fancy piece of work, aren't you? Trying to claim my daughter's honor as your own. Or did this rake tell you he was fighting for your honor, my dear? He's as wild and unscrupulous as they come."

"What?" Sophie's hand grasped her neck in shock.

"I hope you haven't let him sample the goods.

But then, I suspect he has." The fat man leered at her bosom. "But I shan't cast the first stone. This rutting buck seduced and ruined my poor sweet daughter of only six and ten under my own roof not more than two months ago. And he'll be marrying my Penelope if I don't kill him today."

The blood drained from Sophie's head and pooled in her fingertips.

"Lord Tolworth," William said, while choosing a pistol from the carved wooden box Mr. Farquhar brought forth, "I've rarely encountered a man so willing to sully his own daughter's reputation. Are you planning to tell all of London your version of recent events or are you reserving these tidbits for my acquaintances only? By the by, I assume your affairs are in order, sir, to hand down to this unlicked cub nephew of yours?" He motioned to a level piece of ground nearby. "If so, let us get on with it."

"Well!" Lord Tolworth sputtered in outrage. The slightest bit of fear blemished his countenance. The stout man's relations placed the second dueling pistol in his hands and urged him to the starting ground.

"Sophie—" William turned to her. Despite his bruised face, and stitched brow, he looked every bit the charming, roguish scoundrel he ever was, if not more so.

Sophie raised her hand to interrupt him. "No. Don't try to weasel your way out of this—this outrageous affair. I'll just ask you this—did you or did you not seduce the sixteen-year-old daughter of Lord Tolworth?"

William reached for her hand.

Sophie snatched it away from him. "Was this young girl in your bed or not, sir?"

His intense gaze searched hers.

"Well?" She paused; her body felt eerily light.

"Yes," he said, quietly.

"It would seem you are even more depraved than I imagined."

"So it would seem," he said.

"I have now only to be even more ashamed of my naiveté." Sophie stepped away and William grasped her wrist. She looked down at his hand and he released her instantly.

"I shan't defend myself. I'd thought you knew me better or you wouldn't ask these questions." He looked at her with a cool expression.

"Know you better? Why, I think I know you better than anyone, sir. More's the pity."

"All right, my dears, I hate to intrude on this scintillating conversation but there is the slight matter of paterfamilias Tolworth over there. And I do believe the man is unhinged enough in his fear to shoot in this general direction if you"—Farquhar nodded to William—"do not make haste over there to kill him in the proper fashion."

"Right," William said, never taking his gaze off Sophie.

"And you," Farquhar said, grasping Sophie's arm. "If you have any grain of intelligence, you will return to your home to allow us male barbarians to pursue our bloodthirsty sport in peace. That is—if you know what is good for you, and *Romeo* here."

Sophie was still reeling from the revelation of William's debauchery when Mr. Farquhar whistled to Lord Drummond. "Escort Miss Somerset from here, for God's sake. I'll take care of Coddington along with his man."

It was only then, in the eerie morning light, that

Sophie noticed Jack Farquhar was wearing the subdued clothes of a proper gentleman.

William had the violent urge to retch for the first time in his life.

"Steady," Jack said. "She's almost away."

William opened his eyes and peered over his shoulder to watch that young blood, Lord Drummond, toss Sophie's tall and slender form into the saddle.

"Did you remember to leave me something in your will, dear? Your new paisley waistcoat perhaps?" Jack said, tightening the bandage around Will's waist.

It was difficult to breathe, let alone form a retort.

"I shall be wearing it to your funeral if you don't pull yourself together, man."

William raised his one good eyebrow.

"That's more like it, duckling."

"Farquhar . . ."

"Ah, yes. Back to normal. Very good. And here comes Mr. Mornington, looking—well, not quite the thing."

Mornington approached, one sleeve covered with Coddington's blood. "I think the cur just might survive, if he is lucky that is. But I doubt he'll be up to fighting anyone else for a long time." His friend's face was as white as a virgin's gown at Almack's.

William made a decision and nodded to Farquhar. "You're my second this go round."

Mornington opened his mouth to protest, thought the better of it and snapped it shut again.

"Mornington, will you start us?" Will asked to help Mornington regain his pride.

William tried his legs and found they worked relatively well, considering. His head was an altogether different story. A wave of dizziness and pounding pain pierced his skull. At least his hands were steady. He had looked down to check. Tolworth would be a lucky man, then.

"Don't embarrass me again, William," Jack Farquhar said quietly as they walked.

"The insolence I endure knows no bounds, *mon vieux*."

"I love it when you chastise me, my lord."

He turned to stand back to back with the shorter man. William cocked his pistol, closed his eyes and raised his weapon to shoulder height, all the time breathing calmly, slowly, as deeply as his bandage would allow.

Mornington's voice rang out. "Gentlemen, you shall take ten paces, turn and assume a position. I'll ask if you're both ready and you shall respond. Only then shall I count from one to three. At any time during the count you may fire. Whatever the outcome, honor shall be deemed to have been served."

William opened his eyes and recognized the familiar calm, cool detachment he embodied each time he faced possible death.

Tolworth's shoulders trembled. It served the bugger right.

"Gentlemen, commence," Mornington said.

The count rang out and at the requisite number each turned and their seconds moved aside, just out of range.

William stood sideways, making the thinnest possible target. He closed one eye and looked down the length of his arm and pistol. Tolworth's girth made a fatal shot easy enough for even a child.

"Ready?" shouted Mornington.

Each man answered in the affirmative.

"One . . ." said Mornington.

With his half-closed eye, William watched Tolworth pull the trigger without a shot piercing the air. In panic, Tolworth tried the trigger again quickly. In his fear, it seemed the buffoon had forgotten to cock the pistol.

The portly man lowered his weapon, his eyes filled with terror. William held his arm steady and refocused down the length of the barrel. Tolworth looked as scared as an aristo facing Madame Guillotine. Idiot.

William lowered his gun. "Perhaps you would like to reconsider the choice of weapons, Tolworth? Or would you like me to allow you to try again, this time, of course, you would cock the pistol?"

The man creaked in outrage, abruptly cocked his weapon and fired at William without taking time to aim.

The ball screamed past, missing Will by many yards.

"For shame . . ." Mornington shouted.

"Dishonorable sod," Farquhar added.

William narrowed his eyes in disgust, and suppressed the nearly irresistible urge to kill the man. His arm flew out to his side to keep Farquhar from firing.

Slowly, William raised his arm and pistol to eye level and delighted in watching Tolworth squirm. After nearly ten seconds, he lifted his arm and discharged his shot into the heavens.

Sophie settled herself onto the thin, high-backed wooden chair and looked about her aunt's elegant sitting room. An awkward silence hung in the air while the servants departed the room after dismissal. For the first time Mrs. Crosby was without her embroidery.

"I've asked you here as I've something of importance to say, my dear." Aunt Rutledge looked her most formidable, half reclining on her dull blue velvet divan. "It has come to my attention that an apology is in order."

That made Sophie sit up. Her aunt owning to the necessity of an apology? Oh—perhaps she was requiring an apology from Sophie. She slid back down. It was to be expected. Lord Drummond had warned that a scandal of gargantuan proportions would brew after yesterday's show. It triggered his second impassioned plea for her hand during the ride back to Mayfair.

She had almost capitulated. Almost. In fact, she would have if only he had, for one moment, had a certain humorous gleam in his eye.

Oh, it was ridiculous. *She* was ridiculous.

"Sophie," her aunt continued, "it has been brought to my attention there was a duel, or rather a pair of duels, fought yesterday, at least one of which was to defend your honor. I must say, I'm not surprised given the outrageous nature of your antics and the young, hot-blooded scallywags inhabiting town these days. But I had warned you—"

"I realize it was my fault, Aunt," Sophie said.

"I'm not in the habit of being interrupted, miss," her aunt said, stony faced.

Silence and impending disinheritance loomed large.

Mrs. Crosby cleared her throat.

"I'm getting to it, Gladys," her aunt said. "Your impatience is insupportable. I don't know what has gotten into you of late."

"Trying to change the subject are we?" Mrs. Crosby said softly.

Aunt Rutledge blustered and Sophie had the urge to giggle. One simply did not quarrel with Aunt Rutledge.

"As I was saying . . ." The grand dame actually blushed and halted.

"Yes?" asked Mrs. Crosby.

"Well, I suppose I'll waste less time if I just go directly to the heart of the matter. I've decided to leave all of my considerable fortune to you when I die, Sophie, as it seems improbable you'll attain the requirements for inheritance of the Cornwallis dukedom by the date of the final disposition."

"What?" Sophie half rose from her chair.

"It's also in my power to grant you the title to Villa Belza, according to the terms of my brother's will, as it is unentailed property built during his lifetime. But the late duke made it clear that if you did not marry a member of the aristocracy, approved by me, the villa and a small stipend to support you and the residence would be the only portion I could bestow."

Dazed, Sophie sank back onto the uncomfortable chair. "But, Aunt, I don't understand. I thought you'd be furious and would disinherit me. Why haven't you ordered me back to Wales?"

"My dear," the old lady said, her eyes softening, "there have been some misunderstandings and I wish to set everything to rights before I die."

"Why, you will outlive us all," Sophie said and grinned at Mrs. Crosby.

Mrs. Crosby cleared her throat again.

"Oh, all right, Gladys. I know I'll not have a moment's peace until I say what you've determined must be said."

Mrs. Crosby smiled and nodded.

Her aunt sighed heavily and pleated her plump, jewel-encrusted hands. "Lord Coddington's father called on me this morning. It seems . . . well, it seems the young cub—"

"The *bounder,* don't you mean, Agnes?" Mrs. Crosby interrupted.

"Quite right. The *bounder* made some despicable comments about you and overstepped himself during the masquerade. It's all the talk at the gentlemen's clubs, along with the duels. It also seems he lost a small fortune while gaming at cards. His father, with whom I have a—a longstanding acquaintance"—and here the old lady paused in embarrassment—"felt it his duty to inform me and to apologize for his son's behavior. He promised a call from Lord Coddington who will make known to you his apologies once he has recovered sufficiently. His father has decided to send the boy to East India until . . . well, as he put it, 'until the sun cooks the ugliness from his soul.' "

Her aunt looked miserable.

"Don't despair, Aunt. I'm sure I deserved whatever he said about me."

"No, I shan't be made to feel better. It was I who tried to force the match, and I who failed to see that the boy was not as he should have been. Not at all like . . . Well, it doesn't matter now."

Mrs. Crosby picked up her embroidery bag and fished for her needlework. Only the sounds of carriages driving past the townhouse and a distant door being shut filled the silence.

"Does this mean I may leave London?" Sophie asked. "That I won't have to marry?"

"Well, yes. Although you'll have to choose a

companion to live with you after your cousin marries." Her aunt glanced at Mrs. Crosby. "I would prefer you find happiness in a marriage, my dear, although I shan't force the issue. Perhaps you'll choose to wait a year until this latest piece of madness is replaced by a new *on-dit*. What we need to turn the *ton*'s attention is a little kidnapping . . ."

Sophie almost choked.

Her aunt cleared her throat and began again. "Perhaps not. But I hope you'll reconsider the idea of an eventual marriage. Perhaps you have someone in mind—"

"No."

"Lord Drummond? Or perhaps the Marquis Dalrymple, the Duke of Isleton or even, Mr. Hornsby?"

At the mention of each name, Sophie shook her head.

"I'd thought as much, hence my decision," her aunt said. "I want to see you happy again, my dear. It's the least I can do."

Sophie looked down at her hands before meeting her aunt's contemplative gaze again.

"I never approved of the family's decision to ostracize your father over his marriage. You know— he was my favorite. And Lord knows I admired his courage in going against our parent's wishes. I only wish I'd had the same. . . . Ah, well, never mind."

Sophie couldn't get her mind and mouth to function.

"I tell you this because I don't want you to make a mistake that will affect your happiness forever. Don't deny your heart, Sophie." Her aunt looked at her shrewdly. "I understand Lord William Barclay was your ardent defender."

At Lord Will's name she regained her tongue. "That man is a greater scoundrel than Lord Coddington."

"I hadn't known Lord Will was in town," her aunt continued. "You couldn't have found a more elusive catch. His father, the Marquis of Granville, holds one of the oldest and most respected titles in England. He was quite the social arbitrator in my day, a stickler of the first order. The marquis's strange disappearance cast a pall over his family's name to be sure. The elder son has grown rather wild, I hear. I know little about the younger."

"The older brother's indiscretions couldn't possibly surpass those attached to Lord Will's name." Sophie paused. "I wouldn't have him if he were . . . Well, suffice it to say I became acquainted with the man in Burnham-by-the-Sea and hope never be forced into his presence again."

"Thou protest too much, my dear," her aunt said with a wicked gleam in her watery eyes.

Sophie forced herself to smile.

"I'm sorry I never met your mother, Sophie. If she possessed half your fortitude and beauty, I understand now your father's willingness to exile himself from the rest of us."

Sophie tried to lighten the mood in the room with a change of subject. "Well, it seems we've a happy event to plan, one my mother would have enjoyed. Shall we retreat to Villa Belza to prepare for Mari's wedding? And through your generosity, Aunt Rutledge, I'll live not five miles from my cousin for the rest of my life. I couldn't have envisioned a more contented future for myself or for Mari. We shall be everything happy, always. And the best part of all is that I can stop this odious search for a *tonnish* husband and revert to my true nature."

It would be heavenly to drop her mask—although maybe not quite so simple to slip back into the skin of the sweet, gullible girl she had been. No, she felt rather half-dead to the world truth be told. She glanced down at the impressive display of her bosom. Karine had spent the better part of a half hour corseting, powdering and displaying it in all its ample femininity. How wonderful it would be to go back to loose-fitting dresses with fichus. The ladies and gentlemen of London had seen their fill of Cornwallis flesh and would see no more. She pulled the ends of her shawl about her shoulders.

Chapter Twelve

*M*y dear *Lady* Jacqueline,
 I hope you will excuse the extreme impertinence of my letter. It is with the utmost urgency that I beg your assistance. I write in the hopes that our most fortuitous meeting—briefly at the masquerade ball one month ago—might prove fruitful for possibly both of us.

I find myself languishing in a backwater bay area filled with gnats, beetles and bats of inspiring proportions. My lady insists on ruining my delicate complexion and hers by insisting on long jaunts in the most inclement weather imaginable, all for the *joy* of delivering baskets of food to unfortunates and observing nature—yes, *nature*. Hedgehogs, sheep and nest-building birds in the shrubbery are her chief preoccupation during these interminable days when she is not strolling—or rather marching—along the seashore. Yesterday, she began teaching the village school children geography and actually suggested I start teaching the little demons French! The final straw (as you English like to say) occurred this very afternoon when she insisted I attend her on a fishing expedition, which resulted in *mal de mer* for me. Well! This is when I decided to risk writing to you.

Would you know of any lady who might be in search of a ladies' maid? In meeting you, I was sure I had found a fellow devotee of the importance of all things fashionable and I hoped you might help me secure a new position. That the lady resides in London is, of course, a prerequisite. That she circulates in the uppermost realms of society is the second requirement. That she appreciates the artistry with which I practice my God-given talents is the next to last. The final requirement is that the blunt—or rather remuneration—for my genius is excellent.

I have promised myself I would stay in Miss Somerset's employ until Miss Owens' marriage, but not another moment.

I understand Lord William has been invited to the wedding. It is my fondest hope you will spare me a few moments of your precious time for another rendezvous or two. I recall your gratitude during the ball when *I attended to your needs, . . . and you attended to my own—quite divinely I might add.*

Your devoted servant,
Karine Marcher

My dear Miss Marcher,
I do apologize for the delay in my reply. Your most interesting letter missed me at several stops on Lord Will's and my journey northward to the horrid juncture of an earlier scene of unpleasantness. Our current resi-

dence, in a little hamlet in Yorkshire, is nothing to Burnham-by-the-Sea, which appears a veritable Brighton or Biarritz compared to this desert of humanity. I despair at ever laying eyes on the exquisite delights of town again. My dear, dare I say, I find myself in the same unappealing little boat alongside you with little anticipation of finding happiness again?

I fear neither of us will ever have the opportunity to explore our own private Garden of Eden again unless we lend a helping hand to our dear, dear frien—or rather, employers.

But I have the pleasure of reassuring you that Lord William will attend Mr. Mornington's nuptials. From there, it is my hope that we will return to London. And who knows, my dear, there is always the chance he will encourage Miss Somerset to do likewise. He does seem to be suffering from a most peculiar sort of *tendre* for your mistress.

I am willing to let this little tidbit fall from my quill, for your eyes only, to repay my little debt of gratitude. Perhaps you could use it to your benefit (and mine) by softening up your employer to Lord Will's person prior to our arrival. I have come to the conclusion I will suffer from my lord's infernal ability to get into scrapes with the (sometimes, I will grudgingly allow) *fairer sex* for the rest of my life unless I maneuver a love match to keep him preoccupied until he is a doddering, mush-eating fellow. The man is simply unable to mimic me when conducting his affairs discreetly anymore. It is a crying shame. Bachelorhood has lost one of its brightest charmers.

But I must reveal no more, for discretion is the better part of a valet's service.

Until next month, Mademoiselle Karine, adieu.

Jack Farquhar, erstwhile Lady Jacqueline Barclay

It was almost three o'clock, the time Charles Mornington was to bring a large group of houseguests for an afternoon ride to Brean Down. Surveying Villa Belza's sunny sitting room and the magnificent prospect of the simple, stark side gardens and the ocean in the distance, Sophie found an unexpected moment of solitude.

The two weeks prior to Mari's wedding had proved more trying than Sophie could have anticipated. She had thought the sight of so many former friends and her late mother's relatives from Porthcall would be wonderful. Villa Belza was filled to the rafters with Mari's wedding guests.

For everyone, there were sights to be explored, large dinner parties to attend, singing and dancing at every opportunity, picnics and horse riding and walks on the shoreline.

The Welsh, after all, knew how to have a good time, albeit a noisy good time.

What Sophie hadn't realized was that time and unshared experiences could drive a wedge between close friends and family. She felt like a lamb weaned from its mother and the whole herd after the cleaning, bathing and sheering process. Sophie felt uncomfortable in her skin, not raised with the peers of the realm yet unable to recapture the simple life of her past. She felt her eyes fill with tears at these bittersweet reflections. Sophie realized she had become closer to her irascible yet loving aunt more so than to anyone else.

And her indomitable aunt's fondest wish was transparent. The grand dame still held out hope of a match despite her silence on the subject. Only her former ill-fated guidance kept her aunt's sharp tongue in seclusion. That, and the fact that Sophie had secretly invited Lord Coddington's father to the house party. The gentleman occupied almost all of her aunt's time and put a renewed bloom in her cheeks.

The certainty that William would arrive at any moment nudged the corners of Sophie's mind hourly. Charles had alluded to it on more than one occasion. William was to stand up with him in the parish church of Saint Andrew just as Sophie was to attend Mari. She shivered.

She couldn't bear the thought of facing his handsome elegance and sensual, knowing countenance during the service the day after tomorrow. But she was entirely immune to his dissolute charms.

Their encounter on Primrose Hill had scoured her foolish, foolish sensibilities if not her thoughts. It was just that she loathed the idea of enduring his presence again.

Through the large picture window, she spied a collection of riders and a carriage on the approach. Sophie narrowed her eyes to see if she could discern William or Lord Drummond among the pack. The latter had wrangled an invitation to the Mornington house party and was supposed to arrive today.

She had formed the decision to see if there was any possible hope of forming an attachment in that corner.

Perhaps her aunt was correct. A marriage of convenience would at the least bring companionship and, with any luck, the wonder of a child. She must consider attaching herself to someone one last time or embrace the relative peace and certain isolation of spinsterhood wholeheartedly. Lord Drummond was the most likely candidate.

Sophie hurried down the steps of the villa's entrance in advance of the party, grateful for the opportunity to escape from her thoughts.

Mari and her father, Uncle Rhys, bustled from the villa to join the crowd of guests from Hinton Arms. Mari's two brothers, Parry and Bran, also appeared with their three sisters, Sian, Alis and Bethan, in tow. And Mari's older brother Aeron herded his three young children, Padrig, Anwen and Wyn, behind the others. Two other cousins, Cadell and Trystan Owens had gone to the port to inspect and try Sophie's new fishing boat.

Mr. Mornington had indeed brought Lord Drummond as well as his two sisters and two old friends of the family, Sir John Tarley and his wife, Lady Tarley. William was nowhere in sight.

"I'm delighted to see you again, Miss Somerset," Lord Drummond said after all the obligatory greetings and introductions. He bowed over her hand and brought her fingers close to his lips but did not make contact. Very proper. He really was handsome—clear hazel eyes, curly brown hair and an endearing crooked smile. "I've been counting the minutes since last we parted."

Although he did utter the most inane bits of pleasantry at times. "Really? And how many minutes have passed, sir?" she asked. "I cannot allow such a comment, meant solely to turn me up sweet, to pass without verifying the flatterer's honesty."

Lord Drummond grinned. "Why, it has been well

over twenty-two thousand minutes since our unfortunate outing near Regent's Park."

Sophie tried to hide her smile while tapping her whip on the heavy fabric of her dark blue riding habit. "Tell me truthfully, sir, are you a genius or did you not calculate your answer prior to coming here?"

"Ah, you wound my pride. I'd hoped you would assume I was brilliant." He escorted her to her mount, while everyone else arranged themselves among the horses and carriages brought from the stables. "I see by your expression that you'll have none of it. So I'm forced to admit I don't come courting without a well-prepared arsenal."

Sophie dissolved into peals of laughter. Recovering, she replied, "I've learned to value honesty above all things, sir."

Lord Drummond tossed her into the saddle and the collection of family members and friends set off along the sandy track.

The first hour was spent amicably weaving among the open carriages and riders with Charles Mornington offering commentary on the ancient field systems, burial mounds and wildlife that could be found in the area. Eager to see the remains of an Iron Age hill fort at the entrance to the down, the group negotiated their way there, with two riders, Sophie and Lord Drummond, promising to meet the others at the site of a small Roman temple a half mile farther along.

Lord Drummond assisted Sophie from the saddle, and led her to the shade of a beech tree, its leaves rustling in the breeze.

His height matched hers. She gazed into his kind eyes when he removed his hat. "I *have* missed you, Miss Somerset."

"So you mentioned." She tilted her head and unconsciously reassumed her mocking temptress façade.

"I was mortally afraid you would marry Lord William Barclay after that duel. Deuced bad business that was, if you ask me. The man had no right to defend your honor. If anyone, I should have been allowed to be your champion. Why I never even saw him with you and I—well, I was your favorite, wasn't I?"

Defensiveness was never an endearing trait in a man. At least William never— Oh, drat her dissembling mind. Must pay attention.

"But I know how females are—just have to look at my own silly sisters. They'd immediately marry anyone who was daring enough to fight for their honor. Not that my sisters would ever blemish their names, you understand. Mama would never hear of it. But, it's those ridiculous amorous notions they get with dashing uniforms or duels. Little do they know that there's nothing the least bit romantical about saber blades or pistol balls. You're not like my sisters are you? You're not engaged to Lord William—tell me now if you are."

Sophie laughed. "You do an awful lot of talking, my lord, for someone who professes to have missed me."

Lord Drummond's Adam's apple bobbed as he gulped. "Oh, I say, Miss Somerset. Do forgive me. I guess this means I'm to be allowed another kiss? The kiss of such sweet torture that exists in my dreams and has driven me to madness?"

"Now who's spouting silly romantical notions?" She swept her eyelashes down, demurely, expertly. "Yes, you may kiss me, my lord."

Like a mechanical soldier, he took one step forward and grasped her shoulders with clammy hands before lowering his puckered lips. Long moments passed.

It was a pity. He still ground his lips into hers a fraction too strongly for her taste. And she could hear air whistling through his nose and his hot breath on her face. Sophie ran her fingers through his hair and curled the tips of her fingers along the edges of his ears.

He broke off the kiss and swallowed. "I adore it when you do that, Miss Somerset." He had a dazed look in his eyes. Lord Drummond recaptured her poor lips and groped the full curves of her body.

It did not feel anything like . . .

She refocused her attention, making a path of small, sweet kisses to his earlobe, trying to force herself to feel something for this man who might bring her a measure of comfort in the long years ahead. She kissed him on the cheek before pulling away.

It was a shame really. He was her age but seemed the veriest boy. This was not going to work. It was time to put away all hopes of a marriage and children.

"Dash it all, Miss Somerset. You *do* care. Will you have me then? I've been praying you would reconsider my offer." He swept down on one knee, and grasped her hand. "Will you accept me then?"

Oh, she hated to trample on his tender sensibilities. "I am much honored by the proposal you make me, sir. But, I cannot, Lord Drummond. I've given you the wrong impression, and I must apologize profusely."

He looked exceptionally disappointed.

She continued. "I beg you not to misunderstand.

It's not that I don't care for you. I like you very much. It's just that I've decided to never marry."

He scowled, then regained his feet and brushed at his soiled knees. "Oh, you don't fool me. You don't fool me a'tall. You're smitten with that—that Corinthian. I knew it. But mark my words, the bounder will bring you nothing but unhappiness." He waggled his finger at her nose.

"You're wasting your breath. I'm not interested in marrying Lord William—not in the least." She turned and walked the short distance past the ruins of the small Roman temple, Lord Drummond right behind her. She faced the sea and let the wind push the wisps of hair from her face.

She smiled and tried to change the subject. "Enough, sir. Will you dance the first set with me at Mr. Mornington's soiree tomorrow?"

"Hell's bells," he muttered.

"Are you too mortified to stand up with me? I do want us to be friends."

"Do you think I wheedled an invitation to this silly wedding, and left the amusements of town for mere friendship?" He spoke the last word as if it left a bad taste in his mouth.

Sophie stroked the side of his face.

He captured her hand with his own. "Oh, all right, but only if it's a waltz. You dance it adequately."

"Well, then, I'll return the favor by introducing you to three of the most beautiful ladies from Bath. And I won't be surprised if all your future dreams are comprised of auburn hair and blue eyes."

"Ach. Promises, promises. And here we are letting this perfectly good, romantic spot go to waste. I suppose you're now going to want to go back and listen to Mornington prattle again about the driest, most inane historical details."

There was a thought. "That is precisely what we'll do."

Sophie cursed the male mind. How was it that a man could propose marriage one day, and seem to fall in love with someone else the next?

Lord Drummond was waltzing in the ballroom of Hinton Arms with Miss Philippa Aversley. A look of dreamy contentment overspread his face. He had completely forgotten she had promised the first waltz to him just yesterday while he had been in the dismals.

Really, it was almost an insult.

Well, if there was one thing Sophie had learned in the last several months it was that gentlemen, of the Upper Ten Thousand at least, knew nothing about the joys of fidelity and devotion. Constancy was not part of their nature.

Sophie looked past the three and thirty waltzing couples to the beautifully decorated entrance to Hinton Arms' ballroom for what had to be the hundredth time. *Where was he?* Her nerves were as taut as the strings on the violinist's instrument. She'd mentally prepared herself for William's arrival for the last two weeks by practicing again and again in front of her dressing table's mirror the correct yet distinctly cool greeting she would make when he bowed before her again.

Sophie watched Mari, looking beautiful with small white flowers woven into her dark hair, smiling at her betrothed as she circled the ballroom with the besotted bridegroom-to-be.

A stab of potent loneliness pierced Sophie.

Here in the Mornington's dazzling room filled to

the brim with all her family, friends and neighbors, Sophie was more thoroughly alone than ever before.

And by this time next week she would be, without question, bereft. Mari and Charles would be on their much-anticipated wedding voyage. All of Sophie's Welsh relatives would be reassuming their lives in Porthcall respectively. School would be closed for the harvesting months and most of her neighbors would be gone to Bath or Brighton if they could manage it. Even Aunt Rutledge, dancing under the loving gaze of Lord Coddington's father, would leave her. Sophie would not be surprised if there was a quiet wedding being planned in that corner.

She reflexively looked at the doors again, then crossed the edges of the ballroom toward the terrace in search of cooler air. Once outside, she observed the gathering of dancers beyond the terrace doors and forced herself to smile in an effort to shake her depressed spirits.

She must fight the memories, the feelings they brought. She must learn to dispel the destructive recollections of her affection for a man who did not deserve her, her— There, she would admit it. She had loved him. But she would battle her sensibilities. She would find peace and then truly take pleasure in the joys to be found living in a smallish parish by the sea. She was practical enough to admit that she would not start until after she faced Lord William one last time—tomorrow.

She looked up from her introspection on the outside terrace and froze. A tall gentleman entered the ballroom through the distant doors. She squinted her eyes.

Chapter Thirteen

*I*t was not he. It was someone who very nearly was William, but with a wider smile, and long hair drawn back in a queue. But they were identical in their coloring, height and powerful physiques. How could God have possibly created two of them? She was glad she was alone and in the shadows outside so that no one could see her open perusal. She glanced at her hands to find them shaking then returned her attention to the stranger.

Charles, with Mari on his arm, hurried over to this Williamesque creature after the final notes of the set. The guest passed a note of some sort to Charles who bowed in acceptance. A brief exchange occurred followed by the three pairs of eyes turning to scan the room.

It was obvious they were looking for her. Sophie edged closer to the evening shade of a large tree bordering the terrace. Charles and Mari returned their attention to the gentleman, while he continued to search the room. His gaze swept past her, then returned to her for the merest moment before returning his attention to the affianced pair.

Her heart in the pit of her stomach, Sophie rushed to the stairs leading down to the pebbled walkway separating the mansion from the gardens. She could swear he had winked at her.

Several lanterns, hanging from the low branches of trees nearby illuminated the front section of the garden. Sophie ran beyond them, choosing to hide behind the trunk of a mature oak tree. The rough bark dug into her upper back as she leaned into it.

She wasn't hiding, really. She just didn't want to have to talk to anyone at the moment. Especially not that gentleman. Several long minutes passed.

She was behaving like a child. Perhaps she could just creep around the side of the property, reenter through the front doors, and retire to the ladies' withdrawing room. Yes, that was it.

Rolling her spine off the oak, she stepped into the long dim light cast by a lantern.

A man cleared his throat.

Sophie stopped.

"Mademoiselle Somerset?"

She breathed in sharply. The voice was not the same but the seductive accent was. She drew herself up and pushed back her shoulders, staring into the darkness from whence the voice had come.

The sound of a deep chuckle rumbled through the air, sending a shiver up her spine. Oh yes, the laughter was exactly the same. They had probably practiced it in their cradles.

He emerged from the shadows and paused. "Magnificent." His heavy-lidded gaze rested on her face quite properly, leaving her no retort. "Mademoiselle, I understand now why my brother was so insistent I find you."

"Indeed," she replied, tilting her chin up and moving past the ray of light into the darkness where the large black shadow of the gentleman appeared. "I find you have the advantage, sir. I've not had the *pleasure* of an introduction." Her frosty tone was designed to wither.

It did the opposite. "Oh come, come, my dear. There is no need to be so formal. We are alone, and if anything, you have the advantage. If you know my brother as well as I think you do, you have a fair idea of who I am." He chuckled again, then bowed slowly and courteously, grasping her hand in his large warm one and bringing it to his lips. "Alexander Barclay, Viscount Gaston, your servant, mademoiselle."

"A pleasure, my lord."

"Why were you hiding from me just now, *chérie*?" He reached for her face, and before she could move, he had stroked the curve of her jaw with his index finger.

She didn't flinch. "I would prefer you didn't use that endearment, sir." She didn't have to see his mouth in the darkness to know he was smiling.

"My apologies, mademoiselle. I did not intend to offend you in any way." He paused and cocked a brow. "Most ladies of my acquaintance enjoy hearing that particular endearment from my lips."

They were as alike as croissants and brioches, two half-French men of the world intent on seducing females at every opportunity with their buttery-smooth powers of seduction. But she did not have to stay to endure another round with this new snake charmer. She turned and strode toward the terrace. A chuckle flowed from the light evening breeze behind her.

"I have a message for you from my charming brother. He asked me to deliver it to you."

She kept walking, only turning her head so he

could hear her response. "I do not accept letters from gentlemen who are not related to me, sir."

"Mademoiselle, I beg of you to give me a moment to explain." His tone had turned more serious.

Her curiosity got the better of her. She stopped, forcing him to stride up to her.

"I believe you misunderstand the mode of my brother's message. You see, he told me you would probably tear any letter from him into shreds before my face. He entrusted me to explain his absence to you instead."

The urge to escape the presence of this man was overwhelming, but the curiosity to know what he would reveal was stronger. She turned more fully toward him, inviting him to proceed.

"My brother finds himself, most unwillingly I must add, confined to a dismal northern hamlet attending to the concerns of the Tolworth family, a name my brother said you would recognize. There was some sort of misunderstanding or *something very like entrapment* and—heaven knows why—William, it seems, has gained a conscience and has decided to restore the girl's reputation." He shuddered. "A frumpy, freckled thing if there ever was one from all reports. My brother is to be pitied, mademoiselle. He was not in any way at fault, only the dupe of a family hell-bent on marrying off their unappealing daughter. Such a misfortune. A waste if you ask me.

"In any case, he asked me to tell you he regrets he's unable to attend the wedding and therefore the opportunity to fully explain certain circumstances of the past. He wanted me to convey to you that once you are familiar with key incontrovertible facts"—he put the palm of his hand over his face and rubbed his eyes—"you will . . . hmmm . . . how did he put it? You will have a change of heart? Or was it a change of clothes? Whatever."

"I refuse to—" she started.

He put up a staying hand. "Really, Miss Somerset, do take pity on me and allow me to finish. My head is throbbing from the most foul tainted ale consumed at the last inn during a revolting meal that passed for dinner. I shan't get this right if you interrupt me. Now let's see, where was I?"

She sighed. "Something about a change of—"

"Quite right. He asked for one word from you."

"And this one word would be?"

"Why, it would be to reassure him that you still adore him, still cherish him, will still receive him when he waits on you after this vile marriage is concluded in Yorkshire." He gently brushed a tendril of her hair from her face. "I promise you he has no intention of decaying in the boggy north for long."

She became light-headed at the mention of William's sudden contracted marriage. Clenching her hands so tightly behind her until the nails bit into her palms, she forced herself to remain composed. "Lord Gaston, I have never adored or cherished your brother as you suggest." Sophie knew God was just and would understand the necessity of this one small lie.

"Really? Is that so?" He arched his eyebrow exactly as William had always done.

Impossible. Both of them were not fit for the devil's notice. The conversation had become a farce of epic proportions.

"No, or rather, I mean yes, it is so."

"I find the depth of your sensibilities most revealing, mademoiselle."

Lord Gaston smiled and unwittingly revealed dimples on his cheeks that were almost like—oh, botheration—at least they did not have the same effect on Sophie at all. *Like brother, like brother,* apparently. "I must go, sir. I bid you good night."

He lightly grasped her arm. "But your answer, mademoiselle. I need an answer, remember?"

"You may tell him that I haven't changed my mind since last I saw him on Primrose Hill. And furthermore, I shall *never* change my opinion of him and what he represents." Before he could utter another word to detain her again, Sophie picked up her skirts and hurried into the ballroom. The man was impossible. At least he served to remind her of all the reasons why a match between William and her would've been impossible.

To be fair, she must at least give William credit for returning to Yorkshire to do right by the young girl he had ruined. But that credit became negated when he'd fully intended on quitting Yorkshire as soon as he could to have a romantic interlude of some sort with her.

Surely, Lord Gaston had not relayed William's words properly. William knew her well enough to know that she would never receive him again after his marriage, except for any joint visits he might make with his wife, if they ever visited the Morningtons. She would be sure to arrange trips to London on those occasions.

So he was to be married. To save Miss Tolworth from ruin. At least his conscience had caught up with him. Her heart constricted just a fraction. Surely it was her new corset that caused the sensation.

She was *glad* he was doing the moral and right thing. She was *happy* she would live out the rest of her productive life in Burnham-by-the-Sea filling her time with works of charity, and overseeing the villa. She really, really was.

Mother Nature smiled on Mari and Charles on the morning of their wedding. An occasional puff of white cloud drifted across the expanse of blue sky. Four and fifty guests filled the small yet formidable St. Andrew's church fronting the sea. The fourteenth century tower noticeably leaned to one side.

The pastor appeared nervous facing the large crowd. Indeed his hands shook as he asked the happy bride and groom the all-important questions that would serve to bind them forever as man and wife. Mari and Charles played their parts to the letter except perhaps the vows had been sealed a tad too exuberantly.

Viscount Gaston stood in what would have been William's place across from Sophie. He barely smiled during the whole of the wedding and the wedding breakfast at Hinton Arms. Perhaps Sophie had imagined the whole horrid scenario last evening. But of course she hadn't for he insisted on a private word with her in the mansion's small music room before his leave-taking after the breakfast.

He bowed over her hand, correctly. "Do I owe you an apology, Miss Somerset? I suppose I must if the size of my head this morning is any indication. Between the foul ale and food from the atrocious inn and the heat in the carriage, well—"

"There is no need for you to feel remorseful, sir." Sophie led him to the pianoforte's bench, the only seating in the deserted room that had been ransacked of all its chairs for the breakfast party. "Perhaps the conversation we shared last night was best performed in your state of . . . mind."

He was very ill at ease. "Did I remember correctly that essentially you required me to tell William that—" He paused, searching her face.

She helped to refresh his memory. "That I never want to see your dear brother again," Sophie said quietly, firmly.

"Right," he said, scratching his head. "Well, at least he is still dear to you."

Perhaps it was the lack of sleep she had endured of late, or more likely the familiarity she felt toward Lord Gaston due to the extraordinary resemblance between the two brothers. Whatever the reason, Sophie's usual grace snapped. "No, Lord Gaston. He is not dear to me at all. He will always be nothing more to me than a deceiving scoundrel, a fortune hunter, a seducer—a know-nothing, vain nodcock interested more in the design of his waistcoat"—she glanced at the intricate paisley design on Lord Gaston's same article of clothing—"than the needs of those less fortunate. In short, the exact opposite of any gentleman with whom I would care to be acquainted. In fact, you may tell Lord Will that I consider his unwillingness to accept my refusal to see him as more evidence of his conceited, overbearing male behavior, which, you will forgive me for noticing, seems to run in the family."

Lord Gaston narrowed his eyes, and raked his gaze over her dazzling décolleté. "You don't know me at all, mademoiselle. And if I may be allowed to say, you seem to know even less about my brother."

Sophie could see a cold, hard fury building in the brother's expression.

"You call him a deceiving scoundrel. Perhaps he is. But have you never wondered what made him such? If I remember correctly, it all began right here—during a long visit, when he met a lonely female bent on excitement. Someone who appreciated young *talent*."

"I am not surprised to hear Lord Will seduced a lady here. He seems to have a penchant for music rooms." Sophie's face burned in anger and embarrassment. "You have said nothing to dissuade me from my judgment of his character."

Alexander Barclay's face drained of all color. He spoke softly, "Then perhaps I should disclose that this occurred when my brother was just *fifteen*— here on holiday after being half orphaned and left to rot in Eton's barbaric Collager program where they starve them on one meal a day and lock them in the dormitory at night where the older students prey on the younger. He was invited here to experience what he most craved—the affection found within a family circle. And when he was lulled by the warmth and security he encountered, he was then seduced by his best friend's calculating mother, who lied to him, telling him her husband tormented her physically and mentally. Will's tender sensibilities were thoroughly engaged and he even went so far as to beg her to allow him to kill her husband—*his best friend's father*—in a duel." He covered his brow and eyes with his hand. "This selfsame *lady* discarded my brother a year or so later upon the death of her husband. The poor boy couldn't comprehend why a woman of four and thirty wasn't willing to tie herself to a penniless orphan of sixteen now that she had inherited a good portion of her husband's fortune."

Sophie thought she might very well be ill. She

fought back the bile that rose in her throat but could not stop the room from spinning. She reached out to grab the pianoforte's edge, and misplaced her hands, causing hideous crashing notes to fill the air. She closed her eyes and all at once felt Lord Gaston's hands grasp her shoulders.

"Miss Somerset, lower your head to your knees. Oh, don't faint." He positioned her head then paused before gently cradling her against him. "Please forgive me. I don't know what I—well, I should never have spoken. And I've broken William's confidence, after all these years. But then, he never could rely on me. It is perhaps why Farquhar is . . ." His voice trailed off as she raised her head from her knees. Silently, he offered his handkerchief to her which she quickly refused by shaking her head.

Sophie didn't dare speak. It would only allow the sobs to escape from her throat. She refused to burden him with tears or meaningless words that would not remove the guilt he would endure for revealing such a horrid episode. She just wanted this awful discourse to end and for him to leave her.

He seemed to read her mind. "Miss Somerset, I pray you will forgive me in time. I'm sorry my words distressed you. It is just that so many have misjudged my brother. I could not bear for the one woman he has finally come to regard to not see him for who he truly is. But, I'm not used to playing the go-between. And I daresay we both agree I am no good at it."

With a guilt-stricken expression, he continued. "I dare not leave you this way, mademoiselle. Shall I fetch you some water—or something stronger? Perhaps some wine?"

She shook her head again and finally forced herself to speak slowly, with a minimum of pauses. "Please, sir . . . I will be all right. I think it best if you go. I bear you no ill will, and I thank you for confiding in me. Forgive me for insulting you and your brother. I'm most ashamed and earned your chastisement." She paused before continuing. "But, I'm sure you will understand that I'm still unable to agree to see William ever again—for obvious reasons."

He gave her a long steady look then nodded. He rose from the bench and led her to the door. They parted in the hallway. "I am the one who must be ashamed, Miss Somerset. I should be horsewhipped." He turned abruptly to meet his waiting carriage beyond the outer doors of Hinton Arms.

Sophie entered her apartments in Villa Belza and stumbled across the Aubusson carpet before collapsing onto her embroidered chaise lounge. The long walk from Hinton Arms through the tall grasses edging the cliffs had failed to sooth her disordered sensibilities.

Within moments, Karine entered the chamber carrying a pitcher of steaming water. "So it was a success then, the wedding?"

Sophie forced a frozen smile to her lips. "Yes. It was all so very lovely."

"And Miss Owens? Did she not look like perfection in the gown I designed with Madame Roussy?"

"Yes, Karine—perfection . . ."

She could feel Karine staring at her. "Miss Somerset, are you all right? You look quite ill."

She forced herself to hold a calm expression. "I'm fine, Karine. Just a bit exhausted and sad to see everyone off. I think I shall have a lie down. You deserve the same after all your hard work."

Sophie could see Karine was about to badger her with further questions when inspiration struck.

"Karine . . . you've had so many long hours of late, I've been thinking you've earned a holiday. I know how much you long for a visit to town. Go then, for a fortnight, with my blessings."

Her words were like magic. Karine babbled with happiness and stayed just long enough to remove Sophie's delicate lace gown and assist with unpinning the intricate hairstyle so painstakingly constructed a few hours before. Sophie stared at herself in the looking glass when she was alone and fully expected—no, looked forward to—the luxury of a good cry. But, oddly, the tears would not come.

After several long minutes, a slight breeze from the open window beckoned her. She gazed at the sea, and deeply inhaled salt air into her lungs.

It all made sense now. All the pieces of William's life fit together in a sordid, soggy mess. He had once been a sensitive, honorable, passionate young boy. But harsh and evil circumstances had altered him irrevocably.

Mrs. Mornington had, obviously, been the worst influence of all. After lying to him, and seducing him, she had discarded him like the chimney sweeps left urchins, grown too ill to perform their labors, in the streets to fend for themselves. She had been a monster.

It was easy to understand why William had become the man he was. He had been forced to accept the rules of a cruel world and had therefore shown selfless loyalty to a select few—such as Mr. Farquhar and Charles Mornington. And he had learned well the lesson that no female could ever be trusted. Instead, he used them for pleasure, never investing his heart to any degree.

And was she not guilty to a smaller degree of acting in the same deplorable fashion? Had she not gone to London after he had broken *her heart*? Had she not become an infamous flirt, inflaming the desire of many good gentlemen in her zeal to pretend William meant nothing to her?

Due to her aunt's kindness, she could be thankful her foray into the land of coquetry hadn't lasted longer than a few weeks. But William had not had someone to lift him from despair and so dissolution and deception had become a permanent way of life.

But there was still the matter of his impending marriage. Sophie must not allow her pity for the boy William had once been to loosen her resolve. She must not allow the temptation to comfort him, to love him, grow within her breast. Even if the Tolworths had entrapped him, seeing him again would only bring them both unhappiness in the end.

She closed her eyes, shutting out the spectacular sunset of molten orange rays shooting through pink clouds above the vast gray ocean. She clenched her hands, bowed her head and prayed for William's happiness. She would not ask for any for herself, only for peace of mind. Happiness would be out of the question for a very long time. But, still, the tears would not come.

Chapter Fourteen

$\mathcal{T}$he steward's reports were gratifying. Sophie studied the column of figures then glanced at Mr. Gallagher who was studiously concentrating on a mound of papers at his side. The elderly gentleman, his white curls pulled back in an old fashioned queue, finally acknowledged her presence in his domain.

"Miss Somerset, is anything amiss?"

"Not at all, Mr. Gallagher. Everything is perfectly in order, as usual. I see your ideas regarding the summer crops have proven their merit. We should discuss your other suggestions for the next season."

"Thank you, miss." A facial tic bothered one of his eyes every so often, betraying his ill ease. "My wife asked me to convey her thanks for your help in sending our grandson off to a proper school this fall."

"Say no more, sir. It's my way of thanking you for taking such good care of this estate almost your entire life."

"Well, it was very good of you."

She suppressed a smile. It was the closest she would get to a personal comment from the dedicated curmudgeon. It had taken three months, but at last she had gained the respect and proper deference due her from all of the servants. Ofttimes, she hated the burden. She would have much rather succumbed to the gaiety and friendliness she heard emanating from the kitchen and stables. There were few real joys to be found as the mistress, only hollow creature comforts.

Mari's sister, Alis, had become Sophie's new companion to preserve an air of propriety. But the duties of companionship were fairly lost on Alis who, for the first time away from a large boisterous family, reveled in the quiet. The cousin could not be pried away from her books or the solitude of her embroidery.

And so Sophie roamed the cliffs alone and accepted the shy formality afforded her by all the tenants, villagers and shepherds wherever she went. She rigorously shook off every moment of ennui that dared rear its indolent head by a strict schedule of charitable work, landowner duties and few pleasures.

Her thoughts were interrupted by the butler's intrusion into the steward's dark and leathery lair. "Lord William Barclay to see you, miss."

Her breath caught in her throat. "Excuse me, Simmons?"

"Lord William. I put him in the smaller sitting room on the west end, miss."

"I—I am sorry, Simmons, but I cannot see him, presently. I must finish this review with Mr. Gallagher."

The steward cleared his throat. "I can wait, miss. There are still entries to—"

"Thank you, Mr. Gallagher, but I prefer to attend to this now," Sophie said and turned to the butler. "You may tell Lord Will-William"—she swallowed quickly—"that I am not receiving today."

A long silence engulfed the room.

"That is all, Simmons," she said with more firmness than she felt.

He bowed and retreated.

Sophie looked unseeing at the ledger in front of her. After a few minutes that felt more like hours, she rose, trying not to sway. "I think I shall excuse myself, Mr. Gallagher, after all. Shall we begin again tomorrow, say at eight o'clock?"

"Of course, miss."

Sophie barely heard his words. She rushed to the hallway, and turned down the narrow corridor toward the servant's entrance at the back of the villa. Struggling with the heavy oak door, she budged it slightly and slipped past, not bothering to secure it behind her.

She must get away. Get away from all possibility of seeing him. The passionate turbulence she'd tightly leashed in the remotest corner of her mind came unbound in a torrent of emotions that threatened to overwhelm her.

Half running along the faint trail to the cliff and the sea, and breathing hard from the exertion, she tried not to succumb to the addictive notion of hope. She'd not dared imagine he would ignore her words and come.

Oh, she'd dreamed about seeing him again. And she'd woken each time and had desperately clung to the memory of those precious imaginings. She'd decided she had little of the moral strength from her past life. Hence the need for distance.

She glanced over her shoulder to see if anyone followed her, then stumbled over an overgrown tree root. Damp tendrils of her hair clung to her neck and face, hampering her vision.

She chose her footing with more care when she negotiated the steep, winding trail down the cliff. The dirt and grass gave way to sandy loam at the small ledge where she jumped onto the beach littered with odd bits of driftwood. The heavy, moisture-laden air depressed her spirits further. With reckless abandon, she kicked free of her sodden slippers at the base of the berm.

Sophie ran to the sea, her feet sinking into the wet sand and foam at the water's edge. The sea, what she could see of it through the fog, was a deep glassy gray. She closed her eyes and tried to regain her composure by regulating her breathing.

God was testing her. She struggled to listen to her heart, past the erratic pounding. But Sophie knew what she must do or, rather, what she must not do. It was what her father would have expected of her.

She turned and strode along the shoreline in the dense haze. The hem of her dress became heavy with sand and water.

Suddenly, a dark figure appeared in the swirling fog, striding before her. His tall black riding boots left deep impressions in the sand while the mist played with the black tails of his coat.

Her step faltered. And so she would find out if her character was something she could be proud of after all.

William was angry—an emotion Sophie had never seen on his face. And he was becoming more furious by the second if the cold, marble mask he wore was any indication. He bowed correctly in front of her, all heavy-lidded charm, and devil-may-care attitude gone from his expression. He appeared years younger in his fury.

"You will not even receive me, Sophie? Your mistrust or is it *disgust,* of my character is so deep, then? Is it as my brother says—that you cannot find it in your heart to forgive me for my earlier deception?" He gripped her arms almost painfully. "You always spoke of your father's principles. Did he not teach you forgiveness? Is not absolution part of godliness? You are so sure of your own actions in your lifetime?"

She pushed him away from her.

The pounding in her throat made it difficult to speak properly. "I forgave you long ago, William. More than you know. But, you are correct about my old-fashioned morals. I find I'm not made for casual affairs. My upbringing cannot be overcome no matter how great the immediate gratification. I refused to see you as I didn't want to be tempted— for the hours and days after would torment me for a lifetime. Now I beg you to go away from here . . . from me." She looked up at him with tears brimming in her eyes.

"But I don't want a casual affair with you," he replied with impatience. "I never have."

"But that is all you can offer me now." She examined her hands. The starkness of his open expression was almost too painful to witness.

"Ah. So it is true—what my brother relayed? I understand Lord Drummond was here. My guess is that he was sniffing about, his hat in hand and his heart on his sleeve." His eyes narrowed. "You've accepted him?"

Her throat was sore from checked tears and she couldn't speak. She shook her head.

Abruptly, he pulled her into his arms and buried his face in her hair. "Is the thought of a life spent with me so abhorrent?"

Sophie tried to remain all awkward elbows and angles, but failed. She softened and allowed herself the momentary illusion of comfort within his embrace. She held back the tears threatening to spill from her tightly closed eyes.

He leaned close to her ear. "Hush, my love. I'm sorry. I can't bear to hear you cry." He kissed her temple. "I only came to tell you that . . . well"—he paused and added in a hoarse whisper—"I love you. I cannot bear the thought of being without you."

The tears Sophie had so ruthlessly held in check for so many months spilled down her cheeks.

"But I'll go away again if it is truly what you want. It's just that I spent so much time in Yorkshire arranging the marriage for that silly chit—all for you. I knew it was what you would want me to do even if I was the not-so-innocent dupe of their scheme."

Sophie cringed at the mention of his marriage.

He stroked her head. And she remained pressed into his neck cloth, unable to give up the false comfort yet.

"And I did fairly well by the girl. The great lummox of a rich local squire's son, for whom it seems she had a childhood fondness, was thoroughly convinced she was the ugly duckling grown into the beautiful swan after Farquhar corseted, primped and dressed the girl. And Tolworth—a tightfisted man if ever there was one—was soon drawn to the idea of saving a bundle on the dowry. It was a love match on every level."

What? Miss Tolworth wed to a squire's son?

Could it be? Sophie cried harder and tightened her grip on his coat. Vast waves of emotion flowed through her and she struggled to speak without success.

"I'm rambling . . . I—I've run out of things to say. I'd prepared an elegant speech to be delivered in a salon that was to have been followed by you falling gratefully at my feet, accepting my explanations and apologizing for thinking the worst of me and refusing to see me." He touched his hands to her lips to silence her plea to speak. "When Alex relayed your refusal—in much kinder terms than what you probably said—I almost decided to stay away. But, I found I couldn't give up hope unless I faced you one last time. Ah, Sophie, forgive my stubbornness."

He pulled slightly away from her and lowered his lips to hers before she could say one word. And he did it calmly, softly and thoughtfully. Not passionately, not calculated to titillate, only quietly, to express his deep love for her.

Sophie felt every nuance of his feelings flow from his lips to hers. And she quieted finally, although speaking was out of the question. She savored the idea of loving him without guilt.

Time slowed to the pulse of her heart when she paused to encounter his open gaze with her own. All masks dissolved. And for the briefest instant, Sophie looked past the dark depths of his eyes and glimpsed through the window to his soul. There were the embers of a burning need haunting his spirit and a lingering question in his expression.

No words seemed adequate to reassure him. And if she did speak of the depths of her feelings, she feared the tears burning the back of her eyes might overcome her again. Only a forced change of emotion—a lighthearted manner—would rescue her from unhappy reminiscences of the past.

An idea itched the corners of her mind. It was wicked, yes, and sinful, and immoral, and deliciously devilish—just what was wanting and had been wanting for too long.

And so quite rationally, with every thought to the impropriety of it, Sophie unfastened the buttons of his waistcoat.

He swallowed and looked down at her. "My God, Sophie, what are you doing?"

She smiled through the tears, which had all but stopped and tried to fashion a coquettish smile on her face. "Why all this talk of morals and principles has made me remember that I was never allowed to give you your lessons of so long ago." She pulled his linen shirt free from his doeskin breeches and reached up inside to touch the hard planes of his chest.

He wore a painful look of hope and raw longing. For the first time, Sophie witnessed uncertainty in his expression.

She continued. "I was to teach you about *Character,* and instill a *Distaste for dandies* as part of showing you the *Error of your ways*. You remember—C, D and E?" She slowly drew back one end of his neck cloth, unraveling the intricate confection.

William stopped her hands with his own, and stared at her. The burning need she had glimpsed in his depths rose to the surface. He stood stock-still.

On tiptoe, she reached his face with her lips, showering him with kisses—on his bronzed, angular cheekbones, the bridge of his strong nose, on his noble forehead, and last of all on his full lips. The muscles of his broad back coiled tightly under her caresses.

Lightly nipping his ear, she whispered, "Perhaps it is you who should be teaching me about character, for yours—I am now convinced—is undoubtedly superior to mine." She disentangled herself from the warmth of his embrace. "But, I shall live up to my promise of a lesson while you devise a suitable penance for me for—for reveling in your embrace while believing you were married to Miss Tolworth." She peeped up to encounter a look of disbelief on his face.

"I—married to Penelope Tolworth? Who had the audacity to suggest that?"

"No one. When your brother mentioned you were arranging a marriage in Yorkshire, I assumed it was your own."

"My brother has never been known for his clarity," Will replied dryly.

Sophie shook her head. "No, no, Will. He did me a great courtesy, which cost him greatly in familial pride. Although it might be a long time before you see it as I do." She paused, awkwardly. "He had the courage to tell me something of your past—your years at Eton and visits here. . . ."

He grasped her small hand in his large masculine one and looked uncomfortable. "Why, I shall have to fry his spirits-laden liver and serve it to Mrs. Tickle for nuncheon."

"I suspected you would say as much. But you should be forewarned that I shall protect him with my life—so grateful am I for his forcing me to examine my ill-conceived notions of your character."

Will looked at her with hunger in his eyes. "I find I have no interest in talking further about my damn brother."

She smiled up at him and forced back a flash of shyness. "May I then—that is—would you allow me to proceed with the lessons?"

His lips twitched. "If it includes removing your clothes as well, I could perhaps be persuaded."

Heart hammering, she led him to a sheltered overhang in the cliff face, plucking his long forgotten greatcoat from the sand along the way.

Between the heavy fog, and the cliff, no one would see them except for a bold seagull or two.

He took her hands in his own and stood before her, searching her face. The heartfelt expression of joy found deeply lodged in his eyes spoke volumes.

She tugged at the formfitting coat sleeves of his austere black coat. William took over the removal of the rest of his clothes and arranged his greatcoat in the remote corner. Sophie unbuttoned and untied the hidden fastenings of her gown and chemise and let them slide to the ground. Stepping over the puffed-up dress and undergarments, she turned into Will's arms.

The sound of waves breaking and the cry of invisible seagulls in the shroud of fog cocooned them. His beautiful dark eyes were flooded with happiness and longing. She reached up to move a lock of his hair from his eyes then touched her lips to his.

Within moments, Sophie lay on his greatcoat, her pale body almost fawnlike against the black fabric. She reached her arms toward him and he joined her, his body covering her own, the urgency of his desire in evidence.

"Perhaps, I shan't have to help you acquire a distaste for dandies, after all, my lord." Laughter threaded her words.

He raised himself on his forearms and arched an

eyebrow. "I've always prided myself in being a quick study, ma'am."

There, finally, a glimmer of his old roguish charm surfaced in the corners of his expression—or perhaps it was just his dimples making an appearance.

His leg fell between hers and nudged the sensitive juncture of her thighs and he lowered himself reverently to her breasts, pausing to kiss each tip.

She gasped in pleasure and pushed at his impossibly strong shoulders. "No, no, this is my lesson. You're getting ahead of yourself." She urged him to his back and leaned over him.

Her fingers, tentative at first then more boldly, touched the length of his body, hesitating only once.

He groaned. "Don't touch me, Sophie, or this will be over before it has begun."

She stopped, then smiled at him before placing gentle kisses on his neck down to his flat nipple. She swirled the small tip of her tongue around him, then nibbled on the tightened bit of flesh.

"You're going to regret this," he growled into her ear as her face passed near his. "I am going to disgrace myself and act like an inexperienced schoolboy."

"I should like to see that better than the experienced rake."

"I assure you, you would not," he said dryly. He then groaned and all restraint lost, he grasped her hips and positioned her over him, urging her to take him. "I can't bear another moment."

She whispered in his ear, "Well, I cannot bear it either." Sophie sensed the pulsing heat of him and experienced a torturous desire to be possessed.

He drew her down, achingly slowly, and firmly adjusted his hardness to her softness.

She let out her pent up breath. "Oh . . ."

William stopped, and looked at her with a closed expression. There was tense restraint in every still bunched muscle.

She leaned close and kissed the recent scar on his brow.

"Ah, Sophie, you are about to be granted your wish."

"The inexperienced schoolboy wish?"

"Precisely."

"Good. You were never allowed to experience the innocence of youth. We shall bring it back for you."

He closed his eyes and tried to regain control. Within moments a low rumble of laughter came from him. "My love, I've reconsidered." He opened his eyes and reached to stroke the pins from her half-fallen and tangled hair. "I have a reputation to maintain, don't you know?"

Sophie smiled and found herself unexpectedly swept beneath him, his greatcoat at her back. He began a slow rhythm of movements, his actions deep and sure.

When the rising sweet pain of pleasure overwhelmed her, William strained as deeply as he dared, thrusting a final fraction to meld their two bodies together. A crest of pure light swept over them both, and Sophie held her breath to experience the last wave of rapture.

His overly long hair drifted over her eyelids and his achingly familiar scent curled through her senses. She was finally content and at peace.

Long moments passed before he moved to his side, drawing Sophie alongside the strong planes of his body. William flung one arm carelessly over his eyes as he regained his breath. She tried to imprint in her mind the image of his sharply chiseled face against the white blanket of fog beyond.

He moved his arm to stare into the sky, revealing the character lines around his eyes and mouth that betrayed the harshness he had endured in his lifetime. The faintest trace of gray at his temples added to his mystery.

He turned his head to look at her and grinned. "I do believe you have cured me of all dreams of kilts and sporran. Only stays and ribbons shall fill my head—all the days of my life."

"As long as they are *my* stays."

He wove his fingers into her tangled hair. "Naturally, my love, for I have already learned the Error of my ways, thereby saving you the trouble of teaching me. But"—he cocked his infamous brow— "if your lessons are always so pleasurable, perhaps we should begin a thorough review." He nuzzled his head against hers. "I missed you so, my love."

"And I, you."

He gently brushed a kiss on the top of her head.

"I suppose," she said, "we should go back."

"The fog *is* lifting," he said, rubbing the gooseflesh on her arms. "And it wouldn't be at all the thing to have a passing fisherman spot your petticoats flapping in the breeze."

Will dragged their rumpled clothes forward and helped her with her gown. Within minutes, they were clothed, albeit with more wrinkles than before and with color in their cheeks.

He extended his hand in a mute appeal for the few hairpins she'd found then attended to her hair. Sophie leaned back, closed her eyes and enjoyed the feel of his hands working her tresses.

"You've not formally agreed to be my wife, you know." His lovely deep voice made her neck tingle.

"Even though you gave me your unspoken consent, I find I should like to hear the words if only so we will have a proper version to tell our children." There was amusement in his voice.

"*Mon chéri—*" she began.

"Ah, my love, once again, please. I have long waited to hear those words." He nibbled her ear.

"*Mon chéri,* you already know my answer. But if it's formality you seek, then you shall have it." Sophie turned into his embrace. "You captured my heart many months ago, when I saw you—"

"Completely starkers? Yes, you did appear slightly shaken by the encounter," he said, grinning.

"William, that was not what I was about to say. I do believe I fell in love with you when you freed me from"—she smiled—"that torturous corset."

He threw back his head in laughter. "Our children will take enormous delight in the story."

"That won't do at all. We shall tell them you asked for permission from my guardian then asked for my hand while down on one knee and I accepted—demurely and with proper decorum."

"I think they will prefer hearing about your corset." He held out his hand to help her negotiate the steep ledge to the pathway.

Uncertainty filled her when she contemplated their future. "William, are you certain our marriage will bring you long-lasting happiness? I fear—"

"Yes?"

"I fear you will not be happy hearing the whispers that will surround us the rest of our lives—that you were a notorious fortune hunter who married me solely for my money."

"I like the idea of being a kept man, actually."

"You will not."

He grinned. "Well, if your inheritance is the only

thing standing in the way of our complete happiness, I must reassure you." He scratched his jaw. "You see, my family lost much of our fortune and it's always been my dream to restore our name. I seemed so close to realizing it when I met you. Good fortune had smiled on me during a card game where the stakes had been high. I won a small fortune that night—from your Lord Coddington in fact."

Sophie stopped for a moment to catch her breath on the steep ascent. *Impossible.* "So we are now adding *gaming* to your list of fine qualities?"

"Only in the most dire of circumstances."

Sophie turned to continue the climb up the narrow path.

"The fortune," he continued, "was enough to go forward with a set of methodically laid out plans for a wholly new venture—in commerce. My first visit to Yorkshire was to see if Tolworth, a man known for his shrewd business propositions, would invest in a new bank with progressive ideas in lending. Little did I know he had an entirely different shrewd proposition. But, enough said. I am happy to report that in gratitude for arranging his daughter's marriage, Tolworth agreed to a sizeable outlay."

Sophie stumbled slightly and William helped her regain her balance.

"And before beginning my journey to see you, I visited a cousin I had not seen in many years, per Alex who knows her quite well. You would like the newly married Duchess of Cavendish. The duke agreed to provide capital as well."

Sophie looked over her shoulder at him and raised a hand to cover her lips.

"You are laughing at me, madam?"

"So you are now a merchant, sir—as well as a gamester, a rake and a fortune hunter? My father would be most gratified with my choice."

"Now I'll hear no more of that. Everyone knows that a plain reformed rake cannot hold a candle to an unapologetic common merchant and gambler, with fortune hunting and rakehellish tendencies. At least I am not a drunken fool." His lips curled in dry amusement.

"No, indeed you are not. You at least left one *asset for other rogues to enjoy.*"

Slightly out of breath, they paused at the top of the cliff and surveyed the wild beauty before them. Will exhibited his most endearing, wolfish smile. "Speaking of assets, a lesson in the art of hiding yours would not be amiss for I find I don't care to share my good fortune with others any longer." He eyed her impressive bosom.

"I'm insulted. I'm already adept at this art—even you have no idea how much wealth I'll possess now that I've secured a proper aristocrat despite your penchant to join the merchant class. In addition to the duchy and my uncle's fortune, which I shall now inherit upon our marriage, my aunt has decided to leave me her similar riches in future."

Stunned, he swayed in the breeze lifting the fog.

"Well, I see I've finally accomplished what no other female has, *chéri*. You're speechless." She smiled brilliantly. "Perhaps you'd prefer I tell Aunt Rutledge we've decided there is no need for two fortunes?"

"Good God, no, madam. I see we must continue your education after all. Take it from one well familiar with poverty; one can never have too much money. Those who suppose wealth cannot buy happiness may live in their cold little huts. We shall live in bliss—richer than Croesus."

"I suppose it will take my whole life to teach you the pleasures of charity and good works."

He rubbed the tip of her nose with one finger. "No, no—you misunderstand. We shall have the double *pleasure* of improving other lives as well as our own. And we'll also take joy in the knowledge we will have earned a sizeable portion of it in future—by helping others get a solid start in their own ventures."

"And what will be the name of this fine institution?"

"Why, my family's name—*Barclay's Bank,* of course," he said.

"Of course."

Will pulled her under the shade of a large horse chestnut tree and swept her into his arms, pinning her hands to his chest. "I almost forgot. I've brought you two presents, my love."

The emerging sun and rustling tree branches fanned a pattern of shaded leaves upon his elegant features. Her heart swelled with giddy pleasure. "Two?"

"You shall find them in my pockets."

Sophie reached into the warm pocket of his dark waistcoat. She withdrew the beautiful sapphire and diamond ring from long ago.

"If this has too many poor memories attached to it, I shall choose another for you." He kissed her forehead.

"You shan't be able to pry it off my finger."

"You've forgotten there is one more item of importance," he murmured into her ear.

She noticed a slight glimmer in his eye. He

glanced down at her fingers as she searched the inner pocket of his coat lining and touched the edges of paper.

A rush of wind rustled the leaves all around them as she read the document which would allow them to marry without delay of the banns.

"You probably have guessed there is one more fault in my character." He rained a slow shower of kisses along the sensitive angles of her neck. "I've never been a patient man."

"Patience is highly overrated, Lord Will."

"A return to formality, Your Grace?" A certain wickedness lurked in the curl of his smile.

"I am certain, my love, patience and formality will never be known as the chief assets of"—she leisurely tugged loose his neckcloth—"Lord Will and Her Grace."

SIGNET REGENCY ROMANCE

A Passionate Endeavor
by Sophia Nash

0-451-21270-3

Wounded war hero Lord Huntington has sworn off
marriage. But when he is cared for by charming Nurse
Charlotte, she heals his injuries and his broken heart.

Also available from Sophia Nash:
A Secret Passion
0-451-21136-7

The novels of Sophia Nash are
"Warm, romantic, and sensual."
—Mary Balogh

Available wherever books are sold or at
www.penguin.com